Brothers Are a Big Pain!

Kelly opened her diary with a little silver key. Under Monday, August 6, she wrote:

> I've made up my mind. This house is not big enough for both Ben and me. I am moving into a secret place. A very secret hideaway. Nobody will ever find me. Nobody may ever see me again. I'll be all alone. Nobody will ever pester me, especially Ben. Tomorrow I'll move. Today my stomach hurts.
>
> P.S. Brothers are a big pain. Who needs a bratty brother, anyway?

Who Needs a Bratty Brother?

by Linda Gondosch

illustrated by Helen Cogancherry

A MINSTREL™ BOOK

PUBLISHED BY POCKET BOOKS

A Minstrel Book published by
POCKET BOOKS, a division of Simon & Schuster, Inc.,
1230 Avenue of the Americas, New York, N.Y. 10020

Published by arrangement with Lodestar Books, E. P. Dutton,
a division of New American Library
Library of Congress Catalog Card Number: 85-6943

ISBN: 0-671-62777-5

First Minstrel Books printing August, 1987

10 9 8 7 6 5 4 3 2 1

A MINSTREL BOOK and colophon are trademarks
of Simon & Schuster, Inc.

Printed in the U.S.A.

to my mother and father

Contents

The Plastic Pen
Predicament

"Get your hand out of the cereal box," ordered Kelly. On the other side of the kitchen table sat her nine-year-old brother, Ben. "Do you really think I can eat this stuff after your dirty little hand has touched it all? You've probably got typhoid germs."

Ben's elbow stuck up in the air as his hand groped through the box of Honey Crunch cereal. "If I find the pen first, it's mine," he declared.

Kelly's eyes narrowed into green slits. "The pen is *mine*, Ben. I saw it first." She pointed to the picture on the back of the Honey Crunch cereal box. A blue plastic pen that was shaped like a fingertip decorated a corner of the box. Above it were printed the words:

> Kids! Free inside! Fingertip pen!
> Just slip it on your finger and
> let your finger do the writing!
> Amaze your friends!

1

Kelly wanted that pen. She wrote pages in her secret diary every day. She wrote letters to Grandma and Grandpa in Cincinnati. She wrote notes to her friend Jennifer Jackson and nailed them to the cherry tree. What did Ben ever write? Nothing!

"Give me that," said Ben. "I need more cereal." He grabbed the tall box of Honey Crunch and poured out another heaping bowlful. He peered inside the dark box.

Kelly reached for the cereal. She was determined that Ben would not find the pen. "If you can eat another bowlful, so can I." She poured out more cereal and watched for the fingertip pen to plop into her bowl. She shook the box from left to right, listening for the sound of something hard bumping around.

"If you pour it out, you eat it. Remember that," her mother said. She pushed back a wisp of curly brown hair from her forehead and sat down at the table. "If your father knew you were eating Honey Crunch cereal, he would have a fit. He hates all that sugary stuff."

Dr. McCoy, Kelly's father, was a dentist. Daily he warned Kelly and Ben and five-year-old Samantha of the dangers of eating sugary junk food. But Grandpa had bought this box of Honey Crunch for a treat only yesterday, and Mrs. McCoy hated to throw anything away. The price of food was too high, she always said.

"I need this pen for my pen collection," said Ben. He studied the back of the cereal box.

"You and your pen collection," taunted Kelly. "Whoever heard of collecting pens?"

"Only smart people collect pens," said Ben. "Like me."

"Ha!" Ben was not only a pest, he looked awful, too.

Kelly watched the way his jaw moved slowly up and down, chewing his Honey Crunches. His blue eyes stared at the cereal box as though it were the only thing in the whole world. His thatch of stiff blond hair stuck out from his head like a tangled mess of hay. He probably hadn't combed his hair in three days. Boys were disgusting, especially Ben.

"Mom, make him quit chewing like that," Kelly pleaded. "His mouth is open. I'm getting sick."

"Close your mouth, Ben. You sound awful," said Mrs. McCoy. She sipped hot coffee from her favorite brown-and-yellow striped mug and spread the morning newspaper on the table.

"I hate it when he chews like that," wailed Kelly. "He sounds like a hippopotamus taking a bath in a mud puddle with a squishy squashy old sponge. Yuck!"

"Close your mouth, Ben. You do sound awful," repeated Mrs. McCoy. She sighed and turned to the Dear Abby column. Ben's foot jerked out under the table and struck Kelly sharply on her leg. He jumped up and ran to the refrigerator.

"Ouch!" yelled Kelly. "He kicked me!" She glared at Ben and rubbed her leg. "He kicked me, Mom!"

"How was I supposed to know your leg was there?" asked Ben, looking innocent as a puppy as he sat back down.

"Tell Kelly you're sorry, Ben," said Mrs. McCoy. She sipped her coffee.

"I'm sorry, Ben," echoed Ben. He looked at Kelly with a wide, toothy grin on his face.

It was a good thing, thought Kelly, that she didn't have

her squirt gun loaded with orange juice or she would have squirted Ben right on his nose. She pictured the juice spraying across his face while his grin melted away.

Kelly spooned up her last bite of Honey Crunch cereal and poured out another bowlful. She reached into the box. Surely they had forgotten to pack a fingertip pen in this box of Honey Crunch. They *would* forget to put the pen in this box, after she had eaten all that cereal.

"Kelly!" Mrs. McCoy spoke sharply as she looked up from her newspaper. "Get your hand out of that box, and quit pouring out all that cereal. What is this, an eating contest?"

"Ben had *his* hand in the box," said Kelly. "And his hand is covered with germs. At least I wash mine."

"She's making a pig of herself, Mom," said Ben. "I think she should eat that cereal for lunch, don't you?"

"Be quiet, Ben," hissed Kelly.

"Now me, I'm starved," said Ben as he poured a fourth bowlful of cereal.

"If you pour it out, you eat it. Remember that," said Mrs. McCoy. She leaned her chin on her upturned palm. "You'll both get stomachaches. Watch and see." She turned over a newspaper page.

Kelly swallowed more cereal. "Pass me the juice, Ben," she said.

"Say please," he answered, looking out the window.

"Pass me the juice, *please!*" Kelly ordered. Ben reached for the tall plastic juice container and pushed it across the table. It toppled over the butter dish and hit the table with a thud. The lid flew off and orange juice flowed straight into Kelly's lap.

"You brat!" she screamed, jumping up. "Look what

5

you did! You got orange juice all over my new blue jumpsuit." Juice splashed down her legs, across her chair, and onto the floor. "That does it!" she said. Her green eyes flashed. "I'm going to get you, Ben McCoy. You'll be sorry you were ever born." She ran around the kitchen table and almost grabbed Ben's collar, but he ducked, slid out of his chair, and took off through the family room.

"All right. That's enough," called Mrs. McCoy. She stood up and knocked her chair over backward. "Bicker, bicker, fight, fight! That's all you two children ever do. I'll give you something to do right now. Ben, you mop up this mess. Kelly, you . . . you clean the basement."

Suddenly Kelly doubled over. She grabbed her stomach. "My stomach hurts! Oooh, my stomach!"

"My stomach hurts, too," moaned Ben. His face had turned a shade of green. "I feel like I ate a two-hundred pound watermelon." He groaned and staggered up the stairs.

"I'll clean the basement tomorrow, Mom. I don't feel so good." Kelly swallowed hard and stumbled up the stairs behind Ben. She shared her room with Samantha, who had just awakened. Samantha walked through the bedroom doorway, dragging her tattered blanket on the floor behind her.

"I knew you children would get stomachaches," called Mrs. McCoy. "I never should have let you eat all that. Never again."

"Mom," said Kelly. "Bring me some Pepto-Bismol." Kelly climbed into the large double bed that she shared with Samantha. Grandma's cotton patchwork quilt slid to the floor. Cracker crumbs prickled Kelly's arms.

Kelly's mother hurried into the room. She blotted the orange juice from Kelly's jumpsuit with a soft terry cloth towel and then poured the thick pink medicine into a large spoon. Kelly opened her mouth and gulped the pink stuff down.

"I have to get my own bed, Mom. Samantha eats crackers in this bed. I'm going crazy. Feel these cracker crumbs." Kelly stretched one arm across the crumby sheet and held her stomach with the other.

"I'll speak to Samantha," said Mrs. McCoy. She screwed the cap back on the bottle of Pepto-Bismol.

"In fact, I need a whole new room. Samantha gets into my things all the time."

"I know you do." Mrs. McCoy glanced around the small room.

"Dad promised me he would build me a bedroom in the basement. It's been weeks since he said he would."

"He'll keep his promise. The lumber should be delivered any day."

Kelly felt her new jumpsuit, now all sticky and damp. She could hear Ben yowling in the next room like a sick hound dog. "And Ben, Mom. He's driving me crazy. Did you have to have Ben? He's ruining my life! Couldn't you have just had Samantha and me? Or how about just me? That would be the best, being an only child."

"Kelly, you're eleven years old," said Mrs. McCoy. "Ben is only nine."

"I can't help that. He's ruining my life." Tears filled Kelly's eyes. "I need a drink of water." She reached for her yellow cup, which always sat on her bedside table beside her diary and her stack of library books. Just as the cup reached her lips, she screamed. "Worms! Ben's worms, Mom. He put them in my cup!" She groaned and slammed the cup on the table. A few worms crawled out. The rest were dead.

"A fine place for worms!" said Kelly's mother as she picked up the cup. "Now settle down, honey." She smoothed Kelly's short, straight brown hair and hurried into Ben's room with the Pepto-Bismol bottle and the cup of worms.

Kelly brushed the cracker crumbs to the bottom of the bed. She reached for her library book, opened it to page forty-three, and let out a roof-raising scream. "Mom! There is a dried-up, shriveled-up, dirty old mouse tail in my book. And Ben put it there! Didn't you, Ben?" Kelly pounded on her bedroom wall. She hoped Ben's stomach hurt worse than hers.

"That's my best bookmark. And that's a good story," yelled back Ben through the wall. "Don't lose my place."

"Keep your mouse tails out of my library books!" cried Kelly. She wiped the tears from her eyes as Samantha strolled back into her bedroom, dragging her blanket behind her. Samantha had a giant smile on her face.

"Look what I found, Kelly." Samantha held up the blue fingertip pen.

"It's mine," said Kelly.

"No, it's not. It's mine. I found it," said Samantha. She bounded down the hallway, leaving her blanket in a little gray pile in the bedroom doorway.

Kelly opened her diary with a little silver key. There would be no mouse tails in her diary, she was sure. Under Monday, August 6, she wrote:

I've made up my mind. This house is not big enough for both Ben and me. I am moving into a secret place. A very secret hideaway. Nobody will ever find me. Nobody may ever see me again. I'll be all alone. Nobody will ever pester me, especially Ben. Tomorrow I'll move. Today my stomach hurts.

P.S. Brothers are a big pain. Who needs a bratty brother, anyway?

The Cabinet Caper

The next morning Kelly scribbled the following words on a sheet of paper:

> *Dear Jennifer,*
> *Meet me in my basement at ten o'clock sharp.*
> *Very important.*
> *Kelly*

She tiptoed down the stairs and out the back door. When she reached the old cherry tree, she stopped and pressed the note onto a rusty nail sticking out from the dark red bark. Then she hurried down her basement steps.

At ten o'clock, four knocks sounded on the back door. "Come on down," yelled Kelly. Jennifer bounded down the basement stairs, her curly blonde hair bouncing with each step.

"Well, how do you like it?" asked Kelly.

"Like what?" Jennifer's brown eyes were wide open with curiosity.

"My new bedroom," announced Kelly.

"What new bedroom?" Jennifer searched from one dark concrete wall to the other.

"It's big, don't you think?" Kelly placed one foot in front of the other as she paced a straight twelve-foot line from one wall to the middle of the basement. She made a sudden turn to the right and walked another straight line to the other wall. "My new room!" she said, spinning around and stretching her arms out wide. "Won't it be great?"

Jennifer sneezed twice and wiped her nose. "I don't see much now," she said.

"Well, of course not. But you just wait 'til my dad finishes it. This will be the most wonderful room you ever saw. All it needs is two more walls and a ceiling, Dad says. Look, I already have two windows." Kelly pointed to two small basement windows up near the ceiling. "Wouldn't red-and-white polka-dot curtains look pretty there?" She squinted and pictured her new room with wood-paneled walls and windows with polka-dot curtains.

"Oh, Kelly, you're so lucky!" said Jennifer. Her voice rose and fell with feeling. Her arms swept through the air as she talked. Jennifer wanted to be a famous actress when she grew up. "Why can't I have a room like this? All I have is a plain ordinary bedroom. You know, with a room like this, we could have club meetings and nobody would even know we were here. We could play Rick Springfield records and dance 'til midnight at your next slumber party. We could—"

"We could do jigsaw puzzles without Samantha messing with them," interrupted Kelly. "And we could play beauty shop without Ben and Buster Gorden bothering us."

"Are you going to have a telephone put in?" asked Jennifer.

"A telephone! I never thought of that," said Kelly. "I could put it right here on this bed table." She pointed to an imaginary bed table. "And I'll put my new bed right here in the corner and my desk under this window." Kelly marched around the basement adding more furniture and a roomy closet to her bedroom. "I *would* like a telephone," she said. "A red phone, right beside my bed. Then I could call you every morning, and Ben wouldn't listen in on all our conversations."

"I have my own phone," said Jennifer with pride.

"You don't have any brothers or sisters," said Kelly. "An only child gets everything. How would you like to have Ben for a brother?" Without waiting for an answer, Kelly grabbed Jennifer's hand and pulled her toward the basement stairs.

"I want to show you something," she said. We'll have to be real quiet, though." Kelly had a mysterious twinkle in her green eyes.

"What is it?" asked Jennifer.

"Shhh! It's my new hideout. I'll show it to you, but don't tell anyone about it, promise?"

"I promise. Where is it?" Jennifer sneezed again and began sniffling.

"Can't you stop sneezing? We've got to be quiet. I don't want anyone to find out about my hideout," said Kelly.

"I can't help it," said Jennifer, wiping her nose. "I've had this cold all week. I can't get rid of it."

Kelly tiptoed up the basement stairs. She climbed onto a ledge that ran along the wall from the top step to a large cabinet that was attached to the ceiling and hung directly over the basement steps. The ledge was only six inches wide, and Kelly had to inch her way along it, her body pressed flat against the wall.

"I'm not going up there!" said Jennifer.

Kelly slid her feet inch by inch along the ledge until she reached the huge cabinet. The storage cabinet, which hung down four feet from the ceiling, was just big enough for two or three people to sit in comfortably. It was as wide as the stairway and five feet deep. The cabinet ceiling gradually sloped down until the back of the cabinet measured only two feet. This back section was Kelly's special place for keeping her books and other small things.

"I made it," Kelly said as she threw open one of the two cabinet doors and climbed inside. "You won't fall, Jen. Come on," she coaxed.

"I'm not so sure," said Jennifer. She always sounded terribly afraid even when she was only a little worried. She crept across the ledge and scrambled through the open cabinet door behind Kelly.

"Isn't this a great hideout?" Kelly crawled around the dusty, dark cabinet and pushed a few boxes into the back corner. "I'm going to do my homework up here when school starts. I might even bring up my pillow and sleep here every night," whispered Kelly.

"But then everyone will find out about this place," said Jennifer.

"You're right. We'll just make this our private clubhouse. OK?" asked Kelly.

"OK! What can we do today?"

"How about Clue? I got a new game. I'll slip out and get it."

"Don't you think it's too dark in here to play? I can't see a thing with these doors closed. Let's open one," said Jennifer.

"And let everyone see us? I'll get my bed lamp. We can plug it in right here." Kelly opened the cabinet door and pointed to an outlet on the wall above the ledge.

"Hurry back," whispered Jennifer. She twirled a yellow curl around and around on her finger. "I don't like being up here by myself."

Within three minutes, Kelly stood on the basement stairs and handed up the Clue game and her lamp. Then she slowly slid along the ledge and hopped into the cabinet.

"No one saw me," she whispered. "Mom's in the backyard, and Ben and Samantha are riding bikes out front." Kelly stopped talking as the doorbell rang. She listened as her mother walked quickly through the house. "Hurry, Jen, let's get this lamp plugged in and close these doors."

Soon every dusty cabinet corner was lit up brightly. "All we need now is a little rug. And maybe some pillows," said Jennifer, delighted.

"Shhh! Here comes someone." Kelly and Jennifer threw themselves down on their stomachs and peered through the one-inch crack of the slightly open door.

"They won't notice this lamp cord, will they?" whispered Jennifer.

"Shhh!"

Jennifer squinched up her nose and sneezed.

"Can't you ever be quiet?" whispered Kelly. Mrs. McCoy opened the door to the basement.

"Right this way. Put them in a pile over in the far corner," she explained. Down the stairs clumped two men in tan shirts and pants. They lugged several boards and boxes of nails and sheets of dry wall and paneling. Back and forth, up and down the basement stairs they went, huffing and puffing, grunting and sweating until all the supplies were delivered.

"Here's your bill, ma'am," Kelly heard one of the workers say. The door closed and all was quiet.

"They never discovered us," said Kelly. "And they were only inches below us. This is fun!"

The back doorbell rang, and Kelly and Jennifer listened as Kelly's mother again opened a door. The back door was only a few feet from the top of the basement stairs.

"Hello, Carolyn, are you busy?" asked a squeaky voice.

"Come on in, Malvina. Hello, Marigold," said Mrs. McCoy. Kelly and Jennifer watched through the crack. The basement door was still open. Into the kitchen slipped Malvina Krebs, the woman who lived across the street. Her five-year-old daughter, Marigold, stood close beside her.

"I saw that lumber company truck in your driveway and wondered what was going on," said Malvina.

She reminded Kelly of a huge spider. She was tall and skinny with long arms and a pointed nose that seemed to sniff at everything she saw. Right now her nose pointed left and right and finally down the basement stairs.

"Building on a new room, are you?" asked Malvina. Her dark, beady eyes stared at Mrs. McCoy. Little Mari-

15

gold began to whine and fuss and pull at Malvina's skinny elbow.

"As a matter of fact, we are," said Kelly's mother. "Kelly feels crowded. She wants a room of her own down in the basement." Kelly's mother paused. "Coffee, Malvina? And how about a slice of my banana nut bread?"

"Dear me, no thank you. I'm on a diet, you know." Her eyes darted about the kitchen. "It must be awful for Kelly, having to share a bedroom with Samantha. Samantha is a messy child. She never picks up anything when she plays with Marigold. I do feel sorry for Kelly."

"Samantha's not that messy, Malvina. Kelly just wants a little privacy. She needs to be by herself now and then."

"Kelly doesn't like people?" Malvina frowned and rubbed her short black hair. "That's strange. I thought all children loved to be with other children. Marigold plays so well with everyone. She's so sociable." Marigold pulled again at Malvina's elbow and begged to go back home.

"In a minute, dear, in a minute."

Kelly smiled at Jennifer as she opened the box of Clue. "Poor Mom." She covered her mouth as she began to laugh. "She can never get rid of Malvina Krebs."

"Better stop laughing," warned Jennifer. "Malvina's got ears as sharp as her eyes."

"And a nose to match," said Kelly, laughing even more.

"Shhh! She's going to hear us! I thought you wanted a *secret* hideout."

"I do," answered Kelly. She closed her mouth and tried hard to hold her laughter inside. She could hear little Marigold's whiny voice.

"I wanna go home! I wanna go home!"

"I told you we'd go in a minute," said Malvina. "Tell

16

me, Carolyn, who's going to build Kelly's new room? Will you hire somebody?"

"Stan says he'll do it himself. He's pretty handy with a hammer and nails," replied Mrs. McCoy.

Kelly strained her ears to hear. She could tell that Malvina Krebs was standing at the top of the basement stairs now. She almost felt her beady little eyes boring a hole straight through the secret-hideout doors.

"Poor Kelly," said Malvina in her shrill voice. "To think the poor child will have to sleep all alone in that big, dark basement. It's a shame your bedrooms are so small, Carolyn, it really is."

"Don't worry about it, Malvina," Kelly heard her mother answer. "Kelly will love it."

Mom is right, thought Kelly. I *will* love it. My very own private room! She wished Malvina Krebs would go home. She was tired of sitting so still, trying to keep so quiet.

Jennifer poked Kelly with her finger. Kelly jumped. "Let's bring your record player up here," whispered Jennifer.

"Someone would hear it," answered Kelly. "Anyway, Samantha put all my records back in the wrong covers the other day, and Ben broke the needle on the record player."

Just at that moment, three loud knocks sounded on their cabinet door. Kelly looked at Jennifer and froze. Jennifer clapped her hand over her mouth. Again someone pounded three times on the door.

Creepy

Kelly threw open the cabinet door and was hit in the face by a huge balloon filled with icy water. The balloon burst open, leaving her and half of the hideout soaked. For a second, Ben and Buster watched with grins on their faces. Then they scrambled up the basement stairs and out the back door.

"I'm going to get you for this, Ben!" screamed Kelly.

"Oh, Kelly, you're soaked!" cried Jennifer.

"Can't he ever leave me alone? It doesn't matter where I go, I can never get away from that pest." Kelly's eyes sparkled with anger and then filled with tears. Ben was a number-one nuisance.

When Kelly's father came home that afternoon, he walked straight to his stereo. He put on a Stravinsky record and then eased himself into his favorite recliner, put his feet up, closed his eyes, and listened to the haunting melodies of *The Firebird*.

"Dad," said Kelly. He opened one eye and tilted his head toward her. "Dad, when is my new room going to be finished?" She sat down on the floor beside his recliner and smiled up at him with her most angelic smile. He closed his eye and groaned.

"Dad, the lumber and paneling and everything are already in the basement. All you have to do is whip it together. That shouldn't take more than a few days." Her smile was beginning to fade.

Kelly's father patted the top of her head. "I'll help you with the hammering," she offered. "Just don't let Ben do any nail pounding. I want my room to be perfect. I don't want any crooked nails." She paused. "When do you think you'll have it finished, with me helping and all?"

"Kelly, Kelly, I haven't even started yet. How can you talk about finishing?" asked her father. He looked like Ben, with the same blue eyes and unruly thatch of yellow hair. He pulled a cigarette out of his pocket and lit it. Strains of Stravinsky filled the room.

"Dad, you shouldn't smoke, you know," said Kelly. "It's bad for your health. I don't want you dying young like Marigold's uncle."

"Are you going to let me listen to my record?" Kelly's father opened both eyes and stared at Kelly with that look that told her she was only good for about one more sentence.

"Ben and I had some Honey Crunch cereal for breakfast yesterday," she said. She jumped to her feet.

"That stuff will rot your teeth. You know what sugary cereal does to your teeth," he scolded.

"I'll quit eating junky cereal if you quit smoking," Kelly called as she ran from the family room into the kitchen.

Ben stood beside the kitchen counter feverishly working with several bottles and pans, spoons, and stirring sticks. "Want to see invisible ink?" he asked, looking up.

"If it's invisible, how can I see it?"

Ben put a spoonful of cobalt chloride into a pan of water. "I'm making some. See?" He stirred his concoction with a plastic straw. He checked on another pan, which simmered on the stove. "I'm trying to make India ink in here," he said.

"What is that mess?" asked Kelly, peering into the pan.

"Glue and lampblack. My book says glue and lampblack mixed together make India ink. Black, isn't it?"

"Black? It's a mess. That's what it is. Wait 'til Mom sees what you did to her new pan. You'll be in for it then," said Kelly, smiling. Ben opened his box of pens, took out an old green fountain pen, and dipped it in the pan of invisible ink. Then he scribbled a few words on a sheet of paper.

"See? Invisible!" Ben held up the sheet of paper to show Kelly.

"There's nothing there," said Kelly.

"Oh, there's something there all right. You just can't see invisible ink unless you heat it." Ben held his blank paper over the simmering pan of India ink.

"Why don't you just have a ball-point pen like everyone else?" asked Kelly. She opened his box and looked at three ball-point pens, four fountain pens, and a long wooden pen with a sharp steel tip on the end.

"Didn't you ever wonder how people wrote before ball-point pens were invented?" asked Ben. "Three hundred years ago, everyone wrote with quill pens, feathers they plucked from geese and dipped in ink. They had to keep sharpening the quills with little knives. And way before

that, the ancient Egyptians used pens made from reeds."
Ben loved to talk about his pen collection.

"You must read a lot about pens," said Kelly.

"I do," answered Ben. "Hey look!" He waved his paper
in the air. "My invisible-ink message is showing up. See?"

Slowly Kelly read out loud: " 'Kelly is a pig.' I am not
a pig!"

"Yes, you are. You ate half the Honey Crunches yesterday."

Mrs. McCoy walked into the kitchen and gasped when
she saw black ooze bubbling over the top of her new
saucepan. "Ben! Take the pan off the stove! Quick!"

Ben grabbed the pan. "It's all right, Mom. It's only
India ink. I'll clean it up," said Ben.

"My new saucepan!" wailed Mrs. McCoy.

"I told him you'd be mad, Mom," said Kelly.

Someone knocked on the back door. Kelly ran to open
it. Jennifer walked in carrying a birdcage, which she
placed carefully on the kitchen table. A light blue parakeet
fluttered and squawked inside.

"I smell something peculiar," said Jennifer. She spoke
slowly and sounded worried.

"It's nothing, Jen," said Kelly. "Just Ben fooling
around again with his dumb pen and ink collection."

"Nothing!" shouted Kelly's mother. "You call that
nothing? He just ruined my best saucepan." Ben bent over
the mess. He scrubbed the stove top as hard as he could
with a sponge.

"Why'd you bring over your new parakeet?" asked
Kelly. She peered inside the birdcage. "Taking him for a
walk?"

"Well," said Jennifer with a small tremor in her voice,

21

"I wondered if you'd like to keep him. My mom says I can't keep him anymore."

"Keep him? Forever?" asked Kelly. "I don't get it. You only bought him two weeks ago."

"I know," said Jennifer. "And I've been sneezing and sniffling and itching ever since." She closed her eyes and sneezed one large sneeze. Then she sneezed three little sneezes and pulled out her handkerchief. "I'm allergic to him, Kelly. Creepy and I can't live in the same house." She sneezed again. "Here's birdseed."

"Oh, Mom, can I keep him?"

"Stan!" Kelly's mother called her husband into the kitchen. Dr. McCoy switched off his stereo and strode in.

"Oh, Dad, let me keep Creepy, please?"

"Who's Creepy?"

"This is Creepy." Kelly pointed to Jennifer's birdcage. "Jennifer is allergic to him. She says I can have him." Kelly chewed on her thumbnail, hoping her father would say yes.

"It's all right with me," said Mrs. McCoy. "As long as you feed him and clean his cage, Kelly."

"Oh, I will!" said Kelly.

"I can't hear my music with all these kids running about. And now I have to listen to a squawking bird?" asked Kelly's father. He looked closely at Creepy. Creepy's black eyes blinked as he looked at Dr. McCoy.

"Please, Dad?" begged Kelly.

"Well, OK, if you really want him," said Kelly's father.

"Hooray! Thanks!" shouted Kelly, clapping her hands. Creepy squawked and scolded everyone for making so much noise. Ben stuck an inky finger into the cage and wiggled it around. Creepy nipped at it with his beak.

23

"Ouch! He bit me," he said, pulling his finger out fast.

"Birds don't bite, Ben," said Jennifer. "They don't have any teeth."

"Then how do they chew their food?" asked Ben.

"See that gravel paper on the bottom of the cage? He eats little pieces of gravel, and that gravel churns around and around in his stomach, grinding up his food," Jennifer explained.

At that moment the back door opened, and Samantha skipped into the kitchen. She stopped and stared at Creepy.

"Samantha, look!" said Kelly. "We finally have a pet."

"I already have a frog," said Ben.

"Frogs don't count," said Kelly. Samantha giggled and watched Creepy as he hopped from one perch to another.

"Pretty bird," she said, "pretty bird." Creepy cocked his striped head. "Want to come outside, pretty bird?" Samantha opened the door of his cage.

"No, no, Samantha! Don't open that door!" cried Kelly. Samantha shut the door quickly. "One of these days we'll let Creepy out of his cage for a little exercise, but not today." Kelly scooped up the birdcage and carried it upstairs to her bedroom.

"I tell you, Jennifer, nothing is safe around here. I have to watch everything like a policeman," Kelly said.

Jennifer sighed. "Now I won't have a pet to enter in the September pet show at school," she said.

"Why don't you ask your dad for a kitten, or how about a little monkey?" asked Kelly. She knew how awful Jennifer must feel, having to give up her parakeet.

"Maybe," said Jennifer.

"You can help me take care of Creepy, and we'll both enter him in the show. We'll give him baths and lots of fresh water and vitamins. He'll be beautiful."

Jennifer only sneezed again and wiped her eyes with her handkerchief.

The Black Ink
Disaster

The morning of Thursday, August 9, dawned warm and misty as the fog lifted slowly off the Ohio River. Kelly sliced a banana into her cereal and thought about her plans for the day. She liked to be the first one up in the morning. The house was so quiet and peaceful. She walked into the family room with her cereal and switched on the TV. On the carpet in front of the TV, she saw five black spots. Setting her bowl on the coffee table, she followed the strange trail of spots up the stairs and down the hall to Ben's door. She opened the door a crack.

Ben was rearranging his pens on his bed. Three ballpoint pens, four fountain pens, the long wooden pen, and a small blue quill pen lay in a straight row on the bed. Ben picked up the small quill and dipped it in ink.

"What's that?" asked Kelly, walking in.

Ben jumped. "My new quill pen. But it's no good," he said. "It's too small. I can't write with it. I need a goose feather."

Suddenly Kelly knew where she had seen that blue feather. "Ben! That's Creepy's tail feather you have there, isn't it?"

"I need a quill pen for my collection," said Ben calmly. "And Creepy's tail feather was just sort of dangling. I didn't think it would hurt to pluck just one. He'll grow back some more, won't he?"

"Don't you ever touch my bird," scolded Kelly. "Keep your hands out of Creepy's cage. He's *my* bird." She slammed Ben's door.

Later that day, Kelly and Jennifer bicycled down Hopper Street, past Malvina Krebs' house, past Buster Gorden's house, past Jennifer's house. "I've got to do something about Ben," whispered Kelly, loud enough for Jennifer to hear but in a serious sort of voice. Her forehead wrinkled up as she thought. "I think I'm allergic to him."

"You mean like I'm allergic to Creepy?" asked Jennifer.

"Exactly. Ben and I can't live in the same house together anymore. I get this nervous feeling in my stomach whenever he's around, and this morning in his bedroom, I noticed I was itching and scratching. I must be allergic to him."

"Allergic to your own brother!" Jennifer emphasized every word like a movie star trying out for a role.

"I'm going to send Ben away for a week," said Kelly, "just to get a little peace and quiet and to settle my stomach."

"Where to?" asked Jennifer.

"Ever hear of Camp Wiggy Wammy, that camp for

boys, over by Madison? I bet I'll have to earn around thirty dollars to send him there."

"Thirty dollars!"

"I already have a plan," said Kelly. She stopped her bicycle and took a tablet and crayon out of her bike basket. Kneeling on the sidewalk, she wrote in large red letters:

BABY-SITTING SERVICE 75¢ AN HOUR
WE WILL ENTERTAIN YOUR PRESCHOOLER
READ STORIES · TEACH SONGS · PLAY GAMES
EXPERIENCED. CALL KELLY AND JENNIFER, 555–2255

"Now, help me make ten of these," ordered Kelly. "We'll put them in every mailbox where little kids live." Jennifer dropped to her knees on the sidewalk and began writing. When they finished, they bicycled up and down Hopper Street, delivering the advertisements.

Kelly and Jennifer had no more than parked their bicycles in Kelly's driveway when Malvina Krebs came scurrying across the street, her long arms waving like tentacles of an octopus. Little Marigold ran along behind her, crying. Pumpkins, the Krebs' orange-striped cat, pattered along behind Marigold.

"Girls, girls! I read your advertisement, and I think it's a wonderful idea," said Malvina. Her black eyes darted from Kelly to Jennifer. "Can you work this afternoon?" Pumpkins curled around Malvina's legs.

"Sure! You want us to watch Marigold?" asked Kelly, delighted to have such a quick response to her notices.

"Yes. I'm having some friends over for our Thursday afternoon séance, you know, and Marigold does tend to get in the way. If you watch her, just make sure she is back by four o'clock. And see that she keeps her dress clean. It was very expensive. From Ayers."

"We will, Mrs. Krebs," said Kelly and Jennifer together. Malvina turned abruptly and marched back across the street. When Marigold saw the door close behind her mother, she threw herself in the middle of Kelly's front yard and wailed, beating the grass with her arms and legs.

"Hurry, Jennifer. What if Malvina looks through her window and sees this? We'll get fired for sure," said Kelly.

"Want a lollipop, Marigold?" asked Jennifer. "A big red delicious lollipop?" Marigold quit beating the ground and looked up.

"Where is it?" she asked, wiping her eyes.

"It's in the backyard. Come on, we'll show you," coaxed Jennifer. Jennifer and Kelly led Marigold into the backyard. Ben and Samantha were sitting at the picnic table on the patio, lining up bottles of red, blue, and black ink.

"Here's your lollipop," said Jennifer. She pulled a large red lollipop from her back pocket and handed it to Marigold.

"Hey, I want one, too," cried Samantha when she saw the lollipop.

"Sorry," said Jennifer. "I only have one." A dark cloud spread across Samantha's face. Marigold stuck her tongue out and licked the lollipop, grinning at Samantha.

"Why don't you two girls sit down right here, and I'll read you a story," suggested Kelly. She dashed into the house and came back carrying a picture book.

"I don't wanna hear no story," said Marigold.

"But this one is good. You'll love it," said Kelly. She sat down on a lawn chair and opened the book.

"I don't wanna hear no story," hollered Marigold. She climbed up on the picnic table and jumped off.

"Careful, Marigold. You shouldn't jump off a picnic table with a lollipop in your mouth," warned Kelly. "And look at your hands. They're all red and sticky. Don't touch your pretty white dress."

"I wanna sing a song," said Marigold. She climbed to the top of the picnic table again.

"Well, OK," said Kelly. "Let's sing 'London Bridge Is Falling Down.' "

"I don't wanna sing that. . . ." Marigold suddenly let out a scream. Ben had accidentally flipped a lever on the side of his fountain pen. A stream of black ink shot out and spattered across Marigold's face and down the front of her new white dress.

"Ben! Look what you did!" cried Kelly.

Ben looked shocked and then began to laugh. "Marigold looks like a spotted leopard. Ha ha ha!"

Marigold sobbed, "I wanna go home! I wanna go home!"

Jennifer brought her hands down from her mouth. "What are we going to do, Kelly?" she gasped.

"We're going to give Marigold a bath—fast," Kelly said. "And then we're going to pour all of Ben's bottles of ink down the sewer in the street."

"You just try," said Ben.

Kelly and Jennifer dragged Marigold, kicking and screaming, into the bathroom and took off her inky dress. They filled the bathtub with warm water and squirted in pink bubble bath.

"You scrub her face," ordered Kelly. "I'll wash this dress in the sink."

Marigold squirmed in the bathtub. "I wanna go home! I wanna go home!" Jennifer soaped up Marigold's face and rubbed it with a washcloth. Marigold howled.

"We're in luck," said Kelly, wringing out the dripping dress. "That ink was not permanent. See, it came right out," she said, holding it up for Jennifer to see.

"I can't look. I'm busy," said Jennifer. She pulled Marigold out of the tub and wrapped her in a towel.

"This towel is stringy," cried Marigold. "Our towels are prettier. I don't like this towel. I wanna go home!"

Kelly ran to the basement and threw the dress in the dryer. She glanced at the clock on the wall. Three o'clock. One more hour and Marigold had to be returned to her mother.

"I put these shorts and shirt on Marigold," said Jennifer when Kelly returned. "They're Samantha's."

"There's a hole in this shirt," hollered Marigold. "My shirts are prettier. I don't like this ugly shirt. I wanna go home!" She began to bawl.

"Come on, Marigold," coaxed Kelly. "Let's go out on the swing set with Samantha."

"I don't wanna play on no swing set."

"You'll love it," said Kelly, reaching for Marigold's hand. Marigold grabbed Kelly's arm and sank her teeth into it.

"Ouch!" cried Kelly. The pain brought tears to her eyes. Marigold tore out of the house to the swing set. Jennifer and Kelly followed her.

"This swing set is rusty," complained Marigold. "My swing set is cleaner. And mine is bigger, too. I wanna go home!"

At exactly four o'clock, after Kelly had slipped Marigold's white dress back on her, they marched her across the street and knocked on her door. Malvina Krebs opened the door.

"Here's Marigold," said Kelly. She tried not to sound too tired.

"Thank you, girls, thank you. And here is ycur dollar fifty." Malvina studied Marigold closely. "Marigold, your face—it looks sort of dirty."

"It's the ink," said Marigold.

"The what?" questioned Malvina.

Kelly laughed and patted Marigold on the head. "The *stink*," she said quickly. "It's the stink. Can't you smell it, Mrs. Krebs? Air pollution. Stinky air pollution. It makes everything dirty." She looked closely at Malvina Krebs' face. "Your face looks a little dirty, too."

"It does?" squeaked Malvina. She hurried away to look in a mirror.

Drumming Up
Business

Friday was even hotter than the day before. Kelly and Jennifer dragged themselves into the kitchen and flopped onto two kitchen chairs. Ben was busy stirring a glassful of lemon juice, sugar, water, and ice cubes. Samantha was counting her pennies on the kitchen floor. And Kelly's mother quickly slipped a box of something back into the kitchen cabinet.

"What was that, Mom?" asked Kelly.

"What was what?" Mrs. McCoy chewed something and swallowed it.

"That box. Are you hiding something?" asked Kelly.

"Oh, here. Have a chocolate," said Mrs. McCoy. She opened the cabinet, pulled out the box, and passed around pieces of candy to all the children and took another one herself. "You're right, Kelly," she said. "There is no privacy in this house."

Kelly smiled. The smooth chocolate melted away in her mouth. "Mom, guess what?"

"What?" Mrs. McCoy fanned herself with a rolled-up newspaper.

"I'm sending Ben to Camp Wiggy Wammy!"

"You are?" interrupted Ben. "Great! I've always wanted to go to Camp Wiggy Wammy. When do I go?" He danced around the kitchen table Indian style.

"Soon, Ben, I hope," answered Kelly.

"That's a wonderful idea, Kelly. But how much does that camp cost?" asked Mrs. McCoy, still fanning herself.

"Don't worry, Mom. Jennifer and I are going up and down the street today carrying signs saying Please Contribute to a Worthy Cause. Help Send Ben McCoy to Camp."

"Oh no, you're not!" Kelly's mother slammed the newspaper onto the table.

"Yes, we are."

"You'll do no such thing!"

"Why not?"

"Why not? It's practically begging! That's why not!"

"But it's for a worthy cause, Mom. Ben needs fresh air. Look how sick he looks."

Ben gave a piercing war whoop and danced off to his room to look for his moccasins and his headband.

"I said no sign carrying, and that's all there is to it! If you want to send Ben to camp, *you* earn the money. Maybe Ben and your father will help."

Kelly looked at the glass of lemonade on the table. "That's it! We'll have a lemonade stand! The Avon lady goes by on Friday, and the garbage collectors, and there's a big garage sale on the end of the street. We'd get plenty of customers."

Mrs. McCoy sighed a long sigh and began fanning herself again with the newspaper. "And who will do all the work?" she asked.

"We'll do everything, Mom!" replied Kelly. "Do we have any paper cups?" Without an answer, she opened a cabinet, and out fell a tall package of paper cups, some paper plates and napkins, and one can of string beans.

"I've got to clean these cabinets pretty soon," said Mrs. McCoy. She picked up the can of beans while Kelly collected the cups, plates, and napkins. "Go ahead. Have your lemonade stand. It's certainly hot enough."

"Can I be the cashier?" asked Samantha, looking up from her pile of pennies. She loved to count money. "I can count to one hundred. Want to hear?"

"No, Samantha. Not now," said Kelly as she opened the freezer and took out a can of frozen lemonade. "Add four cans of cold water to this, Jennifer."

"One, two, three, four, five," recited Samantha, looking at the ceiling.

"Be quiet, Samantha, you're confusing me!" said Jennifer. Kelly looked at Jennifer and shrugged her shoulders. If Ben wasn't being a pest, Samantha was.

A short time later, Kelly and Jennifer were in business. Hopper Street hummed with pedestrians and cars. Jennifer leaned over a cardboard square with a red crayon. "What are we charging, five cents?" she asked.

"Make it ten cents a glass," said Kelly.

"That's outrageous," said Jennifer.

"That's inflation," said Kelly. "Everything is going up. Lemonade might as well, too."

"Ninety-two, ninety-three, ninety-four, ninety-five,

ninety-six," counted Samantha. She skipped down the driveway.

"You might as well forget it, Samantha," said Kelly. "I'm the cashier. But if you have ten cents, I'll give you a glass of ice-cold pink lemonade." Samantha ran back to the house to count her pennies again.

"Uh oh, guess who's coming," said Jennifer. Out of the garage trudged Ben and Buster Gorden. Buster was a tall, chubby boy with a round face. Some of the Hopper Street children tried calling Buster fat, but never when Ben was around. And it was usually hard to find Buster without Ben nearby. Down the driveway they came, struggling under the weight of a huge table.

"And just what do you think you're doing?" asked Kelly.

"We're having a yard sale," answered Ben. "We have a lot of old things to sell, and I want to help earn money for camp."

"Not on this driveway. We were here first," argued Kelly. "Go somewhere else."

"Make me," said Ben. "This is my property, too."

"Ben, we were here *first.* You're going to ruin our lemonade stand."

"I don't care if you *were* here first. I live here, too!"

"I wish you didn't!" screamed Kelly.

"Well, I do!" shouted Ben.

Kelly closed her eyes and groaned. "You're a brat, Ben, and you're a big copycat, too. Just 'cause we thought of a lemonade stand, you have to have a stand, too. You're just a dumb copycat!"

"Sticks and stones may break my bones, but . . ."

Kelly clapped her hands over her ears.

Within minutes Ben and Buster had spread out their special bargains: a worn-out baseball glove, an empty bird's nest, a book of piano music, a Halloween monster mask with a broken rubber strap, nine marbles, six baseball cards, a starfish with a broken arm, and a bent View Master reel. Buster ran home to get some more merchandise.

"They *would* come!" said Jennifer.

"No one will drink our lemonade if they have to look at that junk," said Kelly.

"This isn't junk," said Ben, pulling up a chair. "I just don't need it anymore." Buster came back, dumped his junk on Ben's table, and dropped two dimes on the lemonade stand.

"It's only ten cents," said Kelly, pouring out one glass of pink lemonade.

"I'm thirsty!" said Buster. "I want two glasses."

"Two?" Kelly looked at Jennifer and smiled. "Sure, Buster, coming right up." She filled another glass.

The lemonade began flowing fast, as three thirsty garbage collectors made a quick stop and seven Hopper Street children came over.

"Quick, Jennifer, go make more lemonade," said Kelly. "Here come the Tweels." Mr. and Mrs. Tweel lived next door to Jennifer. They were in their forties and had no children. Their tiny white poodle trotted along behind them.

"Good afternoon, Mr. and Mrs. Tweel. It's a hot one, isn't it?" asked Kelly.

"Yes indeed! We could sure use a drink. And how about one for Tootles, too?" asked Mr. Tweel. Both Mr. and

Lemonade
For Sale
10¢

Mrs. Tweel were short and plump and never stopped smiling.

"Your poodle drinks lemonade?" asked Kelly.

"Tootles drinks anything," said Mr. Tweel. He leaned over and gave Tootles a drink. She lapped at the cold liquid and wagged her tail.

"Could I interest you in a good catcher's mitt, Mr. Tweel?" asked Ben. "Or a nice starfish to hang on your wall, Mrs. Tweel?"

Mr. and Mrs. Tweel studied Ben's display. "No thanks, not today, Ben," said Mrs. Tweel. "Thanks for the lemonade, though, Kelly. It was delicious. Come, Tootles."

Mr. and Mrs. Tweel had no sooner left than up walked Malvina Krebs and Marigold. "Selling lemonade, I see," said Malvina. Her beady eyes blinked and her nose twitched. "Ten cents! That's a little high, don't you think?"

"Inflation, Mrs. Krebs," said Kelly. "It's everywhere. Tomorrow our price is going up to fifteen cents. Better grab a bargain while you can."

"Is it warm?" asked Malvina.

Jennifer hurried down the driveway with a new pitcher of lemonade. "It's cold! I just put in lots of ice cubes."

"I'll take two glasses," said Malvina. She reached into her pocket and counted out four nickels. She took a large sip from her cup, and suddenly her skinny face wrinkled up like an accordian. "Is this that artificial powder stuff?" she asked, curling her long tongue in and out.

"Yuck!" said Marigold. "Our lemonade tastes better than this."

"This is genuine, one hundred percent lemonade, Mrs. Krebs. Nothing artificial," said Kelly.

Jennifer glanced across the street at Malvina Krebs' house. Her curtains were all pulled closed. "How was your séance yesterday, Mrs. Krebs?" she asked.

"It went quite well, quite well."

"What is a séance, anyway?" asked Ben.

"A séance, Ben?" Malvina's voice dropped to a hush. "We all gather in a darkened room and sit around the coffee table, holding hands. If we close our eyes and concentrate very hard, the ghosts of those dead and buried come back to talk with us."

"No kidding?" said Buster. His mouth fell open as he listened, and his eyes grew as round as his face.

"I'm trying to contact my dear dead brother, Leroy," continued Malvina. Her black eyes stared straight ahead.

"Why?" asked all four children together.

"It's a secret," said Malvina. She blinked, grabbed Marigold's hand, and hurried back home.

Camp Wiggy Wammy

The very next day Mrs. McCoy hung up the telephone and made an announcement. "That was Mr. Gildenblatt, the camp director. He says there's a last-minute vacancy at Camp Wiggy Wammy. It looks as though you're going to camp, Ben."

"All right!" yelled Ben. "When do I go?"

"Tomorrow," answered Mrs. McCoy. "Come on, let's get your clothes together." Ben raced upstairs, and Mrs. McCoy followed.

"Dad?" said Kelly. She lifted the lid of her old school box.

"Yes?"

"Here's all the money I have saved up." Kelly dumped the coins onto the kitchen table and began to count. "Five dollars and thirty-seven cents. I think Ben made about two dollars yesterday at his yard sale. It's not enough, is it? How much does camp cost, anyway?"

Kelly's father smiled. "I'll tell you what. Since you and Ben worked so hard, I guess I can make up the difference, OK?"

"Thanks, Dad!"

"I'd say Ben is a lucky boy to have a sister who earns camp money for him."

"Ben is going to love camp," said Kelly. "He always did want to live in a tepee."

After church let out the next morning, the McCoys piled into their car and drove through Lawrenceburg to Camp Wiggy Wammy. They could see the blue hills of Kentucky as the car wound its way west along the Indiana edge of the Ohio River.

Ben sat in the right corner of the backseat with a headband around his head, moccasins on his feet, and a shoe box in his lap. Kelly was squeezed into the left corner. She pressed her nose against the window and gazed at the fields of corn and tobacco between the river and the highway. Strung out between the rolling farms were the quiet river towns with their old Victorian houses. At one time, Aurora, Rising Sun, and Vevay had bustled with the activity of the Ohio River. Around the turn of the century, steamboats had passed by these towns in great numbers. Now, as Kelly watched through the car window, slow-moving tugboats and barges carried their freight from Cincinnati to Louisville and out onto the wide Mississippi.

Samantha rubbed a corner of her blanket and yawned. "Mommy, I'm tired," she said. "I want to lie down." She wriggled around until her head was in Ben's lap, beside his shoe box, and her feet landed on Kelly.

"You're kicking me," Kelly said.

"I am not," said Samantha. Kelly pushed Samantha's feet away, and Samantha pulled them right back.

"Something smells horrible!" said Kelly. "I think it's Samantha's sneakers, Mom. Uggh! Get me out of here."

Samantha stared at the shoe box, which almost touched her nose. "What's in your box, Ben?" she asked. She lifted the shoe box lid, which was punched full of holes.

"Put that back on!" yelled Ben, grabbing for the lid. It was too late. With one loud croak, out hopped Fritzi, Ben's frog, right onto Kelly's knee.

"Get him off me!" screamed Kelly. She swatted at Fritzi. The frog croaked again and took another leap, this time landing kerplunk on top of Kelly's head.

"Close the windows, close the windows," ordered Ben. "He's going to get away." All four windows quickly rolled to the top.

"Why on earth did you bring Fritzi?" asked Mrs. McCoy, twisting around in her seat. "Don't you know camps are loaded with frogs and snakes and every kind of creature you could possibly want? You'll only lose Fritzi there."

"I want to show him off," replied Ben. "There won't be a frog in the whole camp that can jump like Fritzi."

"Get him off me!" screamed Kelly. She shook her head left and right while Ben stretched to reach his frog.

"Ouch, Ben, you're squeezing me," cried Samantha, trying to squirm loose. She wiggled and kicked her feet. One sneaker flew up and walloped Kelly's nose. Fritzi jumped again, landing on Dr. McCoy's shoulder.

"I'm trying to drive the car," said Kelly's father.

"Would somebody please get this beast off my shoulder?"

"Ben, get your frog!" ordered Mrs. McCoy. "I can't touch the thing."

Kelly gasped. "Mom, I've got a bloody nose! Look, I'm bleeding all over. Samantha kicked me."

Mrs. McCoy quickly reached into her handbag, pulled out a handkerchief, and handed it to Kelly. Ben grabbed Fritzi with both hands and plopped him back into the shoe box. Kelly tilted her head back and held the handkerchief to her bleeding nose.

A few miles farther along, they neared the historic river town of Madison, Indiana. As the road dipped toward the river, Kelly caught a glimpse of a large white steamboat. "The *Delta Queen*!" she cried, holding her handkerchief to her nose. "It *is* the *Delta Queen,* isn't it?"

"I believe it is," said her father. "The oldest sternwheeler left in the country and we get to see it!" The McCoy car was soon side by side with the magnificent white steamboat. Kelly could hear the whistling calliope playing a cheerful tune. She waved at the long row of passengers. She had a sudden urge to be on the steamboat, floating down the wide Ohio River to sights unseen, instead of cooped up in the backseat of a car with her mother and father and sister and brother.

Well, at least on the ride back home, she thought, Ben and his frog would not be with them.

In a few minutes, the McCoys were standing in front of the small white admissions building of Camp Wiggy Wammy. Mr. Gildenblatt, the camp director, pinned a paper wigwam to Ben's shirt. Printed on the paper were the words: *Group Two, Chippewas, Tepee Five.*

"Welcome to Camp Wiggy Wammy, Ben," bellowed Mr. Gildenblatt, a large man with a bald head. His voice pierced the woodland quiet. "Get your bedroll and bag and meet your fellow Chippewas over in Tepee Five. And remember, four o'clock, meet at the totem pole for our hike." Ben and his father followed the path to Tepee Five.

"Your son will have a fine time, Mrs. McCoy, a fine time!" boomed Mr. Gildenblatt. "Our boys get lots of clean, fresh air, lots of sunshine, lots of good play and exercise. I guarantee your son will return home with a spring in his step, a glow in his cheek, a sparkle in his eye, and a smile on his face."

"What if he's homesick?" asked Mrs. McCoy.

"No time to be homesick," roared Mr. Gildenblatt. "Our boys are too busy hiking and blazing trails, swimming, making campfires, learning crafts, singing, and playing games. Ben's one week at Camp Wiggy Wammy, I guarantee you, will seem like one day."

Sure enough, the very next evening the telephone rang. Kelly and Samantha scrambled to pick up the receiver.

"Hello?" said Kelly, beating Samantha to the phone.

"This is Mr. Gildenblatt. May I speak with your mother, please?"

"Mom, it's for you. Mr. Gildenblatt," said Kelly as she handed over the receiver.

"Yes, Mr. Gildenblatt?"

"I hate to tell you this, Mrs. McCoy, but I'm afraid you must come and get Ben."

"Get Ben? What happened?"

"I am extremely sorry, but Ben is simply not ready for camp, not Camp Wiggy Wammy anyway," continued Mr. Gildenblatt.

"What do you mean?"

"You see, Ben refuses to follow camp rules. We are very strict about camp rules."

"What has he done?" asked Mrs. McCoy.

"What, Mom, what?" cried Kelly.

"Shhh!"

"First he found a love letter, which belonged to his counselor, and posted it for public reading on the wall of the latrine. Then at supper last night, he filled a balloon with vegetable soup, climbed to the mess-hall roof, and dropped it on his counselor's head. And then he put a frog into his counselor's sleeping bag and scared him out of his socks. I don't think Ben likes his counselor."

"I see," said Mrs. McCoy.

"All night long, Ben led the boys in Tepee Five in singing 'Ninety-nine Bottles of Beer on the Wall,' even though the counselor told him to be quiet. And at the wiener roast this afternoon, he poked his counselor in the pants with a hot marshmallow on a stick."

"He didn't!"

"He did. He swears that was an accident, but the counselor is furious." Mr. Gildenblatt cleared his throat. "You must understand, Mrs. McCoy. A good counselor is hard to find these days. Ben's counselor says either Ben goes or he goes. I'm afraid Ben must return home until he is a bit more mature. Your money will be refunded."

"I understand," said Kelly's mother. "We'll be right over to get him. Tell Ben to be ready."

"Oh no!" cried Kelly, after her mother hung up the

receiver. "Don't tell me Ben has been kicked out of camp! What did he do?"

"Everything," said Mrs. McCoy. "I'll tell you about it in the car."

Late that night, after Ben, Samantha, and Kelly had all climbed into their beds, Kelly opened her diary. She turned her back to Samantha and wrote under Monday, August 13:

> The thirteenth *is* an unlucky day! Ben is back home after only one day at camp. He says camp was stupid, his counselor was a vampire in disguise, and the vegetable soup tasted like ground-up grasshoppers. How does Ben know what grasshoppers taste like anyway? His counselor is lucky. He only had to put up with Ben for one day. I'm stuck with him all the time. Help!

Kelly closed her diary and locked it. She looked up and saw her grandfather and grandmother smiling at her from a picture sitting on her dresser. Suddenly she thought of another plan. And this plan, she knew, could not fail.

Off to Cincinnati

The next day Jennifer ran over to Kelly's yard wearing her bathing suit and carrying her beach towel. "I counted on my calendar, Kelly. Only fifteen more days 'til school!"

Jennifer and Kelly both liked school. They especially enjoyed the first day of school, when they wore their new shoes and new clothes, met their teacher, and went shopping for notebooks, pencils, and schoolbags. "It's hot today. Let's go swimming while we can, OK?"

"Sounds good to me! Let me get my suit on," answered Kelly. Soon the girls were laughing and splashing in the McCoys' aboveground pool.

The sun felt hot. The garden was alive with rich August colors. A patch of ripe corn stood tall in the far corner of the yard. Crickets, frogs, locusts, and katydids hummed and buzzed in the woods behind the yard.

"Here, catch!" Kelly tossed a beach ball to Jennifer. They both jumped high in the air and came down with a splash.

"Hey, toss me the ball," yelled Ben, racing through the yard in bright red swimming trunks. Buster charged along behind Ben. The boys climbed the ladder and jumped into the water. They popped to the surface like corks. "Come on, toss us the ball," begged Ben.

"We had it first, Ben," said Kelly.

"Want to play Duck the Monster?" asked Ben. He smacked the water with his hands.

"No, Ben, we don't want to play Duck the Monster, do we, Jennifer?" Kelly reached for the ball as Jennifer threw it. Buster lurched forward and grabbed it away from Kelly.

"Got it!" he yelled. The beach ball sailed through the air to Ben.

"Give us back our ball!" ordered Kelly.

"Lose your ball?" asked Ben, grinning. He suddenly dived forward and tackled Kelly around her neck, dragging her underwater. She kicked and pushed and came up spluttering, only to go down again as Ben grabbed her ankle and held on as tightly as a cowboy on a bucking bronco.

Kelly finally kicked her way free. She wiped the water from her face. "You little brat, Ben. Here, keep the dumb old ball."

Ben and Buster took turns trying to sit on the bobbing ball as Kelly and Jennifer climbed the ladder and stomped to their beach towels. "We'll fix you!" shouted Kelly. "We're getting the last two Popsicles."

With that, Kelly and Jennifer wrapped their towels around them as if they were caterpillars in cocoons and ran inside to the refrigerator. They opened the freezer door. The Popsicle box was still there, but empty.

Samantha skipped through the kitchen. "Popsicles are all gone," she said. "I already looked." She skipped out the back door.

"That Ben! He eats everything! He gets all the good stuff."

"I'll be back, Kelly. I'm going home to change. Let's play in our clubhouse when I get back."

After Jennifer had closed the door, Kelly looked at the telephone and shivered. I'm going to do it, she thought. I can't take that Ben anymore. She picked up the receiver and carefully dialed the number to Cincinnati, twenty miles away, across the Indiana-Ohio state line.

"Hello," answered Kelly's grandmother.

"Hi, Grandma!"

"Why, Kelly, how's my little girl?" Grandma sounded so pleased.

"Fine, Grandma. How's Grandpa?"

"Oh, Grandpa's outside painting the house. I was just fixing some iced tea for us."

"Grandma, I'm calling about Ben."

"About Ben?"

"See, Grandma, he just sits around the house moping and saying, 'What's there to do? What's there to do?' It must be the end-of-summer blahs. He keeps talking about how much he wants to go visit you and Grandpa. I think he wants to go fishing some more." Kelly paused. "Do you think Ben could come visit you, Grandma, for maybe about two weeks? I bet it would cheer him up." Kelly crossed her fingers and held her breath.

"Ben wants to come for a visit?" Grandma sounded delighted. "Why, that would be wonderful, just wonderful. He could help Grandpa paint the house, and I'll bake him his favorite peanut butter cookies." She shouted out a window to Grandpa, "Jim, Ben's coming for a visit!"

"Grandma?" said Kelly. "We're going shopping in Cincinnati tonight after dinner. We'll drop him off then."

"We'll be looking for you, honey."

"Good-bye."

That night at dinner Kelly had a hard time eating her pork chop. She stirred her fork around in the tomato sauce. Finally she smiled and said, "I have some real good news. Especially for Ben." The drop of a crumb could have been heard as everyone turned to look at her. "I called Grandma today. I told her Ben wanted to visit them —for two weeks."

"You what?" shouted Ben, almost choking. "I never said I wanted to go visit them for two weeks!"

"Keep your voice down, Ben," said Kelly's father. He turned to Kelly. "Why did you tell Grandma such a thing? Ben never said that, did he?"

"Gosh, Dad, I thought Ben would enjoy going fishing with Grandpa and helping him paint their house and—"

"But, Kelly, that's for Ben to decide. Not you," said her father with a stern voice.

"I don't wanna go," Ben protested. "Buster and I are making an Indian trail back in the woods. I never said I wanted to go."

"You better call Grandma back right now, Kelly, before it's too late, and tell her the truth," said Dr. McCoy.

"But Dad, I didn't lie. . . ." Kelly looked into her father's blue eyes and hung her head. "Well, I guess I did lie, just a little."

"Stan," said Kelly's mother, "we *can't* call Grandma back and tell her Ben doesn't want to come. You know how she loves the children. That would hurt her feelings terribly!"

Kelly's father rubbed his chin and thought. "Yes, it really would."

"Oh, well. I guess I wouldn't mind going fishing, Dad," said Ben. "And Grandma's cookies are the best. But two weeks? Not two weeks. I have to finish my Indian trail before school starts."

"I think Grandpa could use Ben's help with that house-painting job," Kelly offered.

"Be quiet, would you?" snapped Ben.

Dr. McCoy looked at Kelly with his I'm-upset-with-you look.

"You never should have called Grandma—you know that, don't you, Kelly?"

Kelly studied her pork chop. "I suppose so, Dad."

"You never should have made up a story like that. You know that's lying, don't you?"

"I guess so, Dad." She wished Ben wasn't looking at her.

"But, Stan," interrupted Kelly's mother. "What will Grandma say if we tell her Ben won't come? We can't do that." She turned to Ben. "What do you say, Ben? Wouldn't you love to visit Grandma and Grandpa for a little while? You might even talk Grandpa into going fishing every day."

"Hey!" yelled Ben. "I'll go! There's a Reds game Thursday, and I bet Grandpa'll take me!"

Kelly tried not to smile. Her plan had gone perfectly.

53

Of course, she would have to be extraspecial nice to her father for a while until he forgot her little trick. But now even her father could play his records in peace, without having to listen to Ben howling like a coyote, which was what he did every time Dr. McCoy played Mozart.

The next day it rained all afternoon. Kelly carried Creepy's cage down the stairs and put it on a table in the corner of the family room. After sliding clean gravel paper into the cage, she washed his water and food bowls and refilled them with fresh water and birdseed. She stirred in a spoonful of seed treat with vitamins.

"Pretty bird, hello, hello, hello, hello," she said, trying to teach Creepy to talk. She put her hand in his cage and held out her finger. He nibbled it with his beak and stepped onto it with his tiny feet. "Pretty bird, hello, hello, hello," said Kelly again, but Creepy only cocked his head to the side.

Kelly wondered if Ben had gone fishing all day in the rain. She knew he couldn't have done any painting. She thought of Grandma's cookies. Maybe she should have visited her grandparents and left Ben at home. But it was nice to have the whole house so peaceful. It was nice to read her book without Ben asking her questions. It was nice to work on her stamp album without Ben turning on the fan and blowing all her stamps around. It was nice to get two pieces of apple pie for dessert without having to fight for the last piece.

As Kelly listened to Creepy's chattering, the front door opened and down the hall came Ben, followed by Grandma and Grandpa.

Kelly's mother put down her magazine and stood up. "Mom! Dad! Come for a visit so soon?"

"Well, we'll stay for a little while," said Grandma, putting her handbag beside the sofa, "but the reason we came is to bring Ben back."

"Bring Ben back?" asked Kelly, a little too loudly.

Ben tossed his suitcase on the floor and flopped onto the sofa. "I've got the creeping fungus," he said.

"The creeping fungus?" cried Kelly. She stared at Ben. Sure enough, his face, neck, and arms were covered with ugly pink splotches. "The creeping fungus! Dad, did you hear that?" Dr. McCoy leaned over and examined Ben's face.

"Settle down," drawled Grandpa. Grandpa was a big man with bushy white hair. He always talked in a slow, easygoing style. "There's nothin' wrong with this boy here that a week in bed won't fix. The boy's got the chicken pox, that's what he's got—the chicken pox."

Mrs. McCoy felt Ben's forehead with the back of her hand. "Now, Carolyn," said Grandpa. "You know we'd love to have Ben stay with us for a while. But what with these chicken pox and all, we thought he needed his mom, not us."

"You did the right thing bringing him back," said Kelly's mother. She turned to Ben. "You hop into bed, Ben. I'll be in in one minute." She and Grandma walked to the kitchen to put on a fresh pot of coffee.

"It's been a while," chuckled Grandma, "since I've had to nurse the chicken pox."

Kelly backed away from Ben. "You better get in bed, Ben. You look sick," she said.

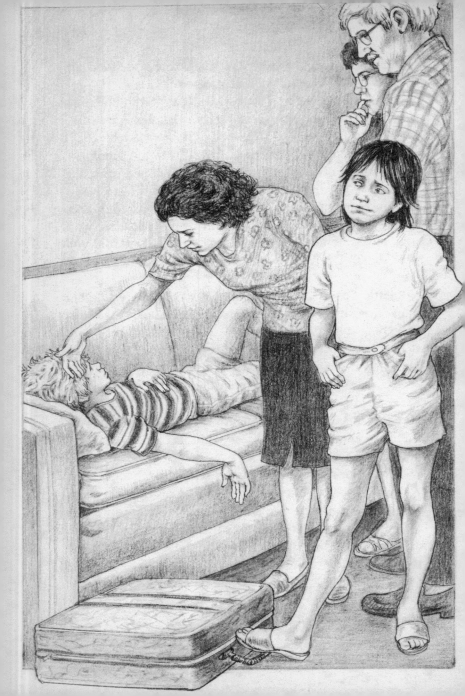

"I *feel* sick. But don't let them kid you," he whispered. "I've got the creeping fungus. I feel it in my bones." He hopped off the sofa and ran up the stairs. Creepy fussed as Kelly grabbed the birdcage and followed Ben.

"Don't get too near me," she warned. "Chicken pox is contagious."

"The creeping fungus is contagious. Anything I touch will be contaminated!" He darted into Kelly's room and picked up her stamp album.

"Don't touch that!" said Kelly. "I don't want your germs." But it was too late. Ben touched a book with his spotty hand. He touched her comb. He ran about the room touching her records, her shoes, her old doll, her pen. Then he saw Creepy.

"No, Ben, no!" cried Kelly, holding the birdcage behind her. But she might as well have been talking to a telephone pole. Ben opened the cage and touched the fluttering and squawking parakeet.

"Now," said Ben, looking at Kelly, "you're next."

The Chicken Pox Plot

Exactly two weeks later, the schools opened their doors for the first day of classes in Lawrenceburg. Kelly was sitting up in bed, with a thermometer in her mouth. She had a terrible headache and she itched all over. Even her eyelids itched.

Dr. Pratt pulled the thermometer from her mouth. "No doubt about it, Mrs. McCoy," he said. "Kelly has the chicken pox. I'll leave these antihistamines with you. Clip her fingernails short, and apply calamine lotion to the rash when the itching is unbearable."

"I will, Doctor, thank you." She walked Dr. Pratt to the door. "I appreciate your stopping by on your way to the office. And thanks for the job offer. I'll certainly consider it."

Kelly leaned over her desk and rapped on the window. Jennifer waved and smiled as she hurried down the street to the school bus stop. She was wearing her new shoes, new blue corduroy slacks, and a new yellow blouse.

The Krebs' front door opened, and out skipped Marigold with a ruffly pink dress on. This was Marigold and Samantha's first day in kindergarten. Samantha and Ben soon joined the stream of Hopper Street children headed for the bus stop.

"How could Ben do this to me?" Kelly cried out. Her voice seemed to bounce around, unheard, in the quiet house. "It's not fair! Chicken pox on the very first day of school!" she wailed, hoping her mother would hear. Her green eyes glistened with tears. "Now I'll be a week behind. I'll get the worst seat in the class," she sobbed.

Her mother hurried into her room with a bottle of calamine lotion and a huge smile on her face. "What's so funny?" cried Kelly. "Do I look that funny?" She rubbed her wet cheeks and then scratched her shoulder. She felt like one giant mosquito bite.

Mrs. McCoy couldn't keep from laughing. "I'm so excited, Kelly! You'll never guess! Dr. Pratt wants me to work for him as his receptionist five days a week. And I'm going to do it!"

"You're going to work?" Kelly asked in a weak voice. "You can't leave me now, Mom!"

"Oh not now, not right away. I'll wait until you're over the chicken pox. But after that, it's off to school for you and off to work for me." Mrs. McCoy seemed almost to fly about the room.

Kelly felt strangely sad. "Don't you like being home with me, Mom?"

"Well, of course I do, Kelly. But you and Ben and even Samantha are all in school now, and I feel like—well, like I need a change, something new and different to do. Something just for me. You see?"

"When will you get home?" asked Kelly.

"Probably just after five. I thought I'd ask Mrs. Tweel to watch Samantha every afternoon. You and Ben can go to her house for an hour after school," said Kelly's mother. She pulled up Kelly's pajama top and dabbed cool calamine lotion on her itchy back.

"Things are always changing. They never stay the same, do they, Mom?"

"Don't worry, Kelly. I'll be home every night, like always, for dinner." She smiled. "You know, you're old enough to make dinner for our family now and then. How would you like that? Anything you want."

"Anything I want? I'd like that!"

A knock sounded on the front door. Without waiting for an answer, Malvina Krebs pushed open the door and walked inside. "Carolyn! Are you home?" she sang out in her shrill voice.

"I'm in Kelly's room."

Malvina whisked up the stairs and stopped short in the bedroom doorway. "I noticed Kelly wasn't at the bus stop this morning. Is she sick? Goodness!" she exclaimed, looking at Kelly. Her long nose began to twitch. "She looks awful!"

"Chicken pox, Malvina," said Mrs. McCoy. "That's all."

"Dear me, I suppose poor little Marigold will be next. I hate to think of all those horrible pockmarks scarring Marigold's little face." She glanced around Kelly's room. "I can't believe my baby is already in school," she continued. "Whatever am I going to do with myself?" She stared at Kelly's mother.

"Get a job?" suggested Mrs. McCoy. "I'm going to

60

work for Dr. Pratt. He needs a receptionist." Kelly could tell by the look in her mother's eye that she was proud and happy.

"You're not!" gasped Malvina. "I would *never* leave my little Marigold!"

"I'm not leaving my kids, Malvina. I'll be at work while they're in school. It'll be a good change of pace, something just for myself." Mrs. McCoy winked at Kelly, and Kelly winked back.

Malvina's snoopy eyes were busy examining the bedroom from corner to corner. She stared with disgust at a row of Samantha's favorite picture books. "I don't know what Marigold would do without me, Carolyn. Why, just in the past month, I taught that child how to read! Isn't that amazing?"

"Amazing. Say, I really must get this house cleaned up. As much as I hate housework, it does have to be done." Kelly's mother walked to the doorway of Kelly's room and reached for the doorknob.

"I have to go," said Malvina. "I think I'll bake a German chocolate cake for Marigold. She loves German chocolate cakes." Malvina slipped out of Kelly's room, and Mrs. McCoy pulled the door closed.

Kelly skipped breakfast that day. Her stomach hurt, her head hurt, and every inch of her body itched as though a million hungry mosquitoes had bitten *her* for their breakfast. She sat at her desk by the window and watched as Malvina swept her front sidewalk and her porch. She swept her driveway even though it didn't need to be swept. Her short black hair shone in the sunlight. Her skinny arms held the broom in such a way that, for a moment,

Kelly thought Malvina Krebs looked just like a witch. All she needed was a tall, pointed hat to match her sharp nose.

Kelly picked up her library book, *Witchcraft and Magic.* Could it be, she wondered, that witches did not necessarily wear black, pointed hats and long black capes? Could witches possibly look just like everybody else? Could witches really cast magical spells and put hexes on people? Could there be strange things in this world that could not be explained?

Kelly glanced again out her bedroom window. Malvina stood next to her broom, her long nose pointed toward the bus stop. Could it be, Kelly wondered, that Malvina Krebs was really a witch? She had often heard strange rumors about Malvina. Some children called her a witch because of the séances she held on Thursdays.

There was only one way to find out, Kelly decided. She would have to pay Malvina a visit. Maybe she could even ask Malvina to put a hex on Ben. Now there was an idea! Maybe Malvina could change Ben into something or even make him disappear! Kelly shivered all over with the very thought.

Ben *was* terrible, she reasoned. Nobody should have a brother like Ben. After all, he was the one who had given her these itchy chicken pox and made her miss the first week of school. Kelly scratched her head and her neck and her arms. This plan just might work, she thought. It would serve Ben right.

Late that afternoon, after all the Hopper Street children had poured out of the school bus, Ben walked into Kelly's room carrying a tattered box of Monopoly.

"Mom says I have to play Monopoly with you," he said, dropping the box on a table near Kelly's bed.

"I don't want to play," said Kelly.

"How come?"

"You know very well why, Ben. You cheat too much."

"I do not cheat," stated Ben. "What're you talking about? I *never* cheat!"

"Ha! Don't make me laugh! You never want to play anything unless you win. And if you can't win, you cheat."

"I do not cheat," said Ben again. He was busy counting out the money and spreading out the rumpled deed cards. He placed the little silver ship on GO. "Are you gonna play or aren't you?"

"Oh, I guess," sighed Kelly, reaching for the tiny thimble. On the fourth trip around the board, Kelly, who owned Park Place, landed on Boardwalk. "I'll buy it!" she shouted, clapping her hands.

"You can't," said Ben.

"Why not?"

"I own it!"

"Since when?" Kelly asked.

"I bought it! I bought it! I'm the banker, I should know," said Ben, waving the Boardwalk deed in the air.

"You never bought it. Ben, you're cheating again!" cried Kelly.

Ben jumped up, threw the Boardwalk deed on the table, and stomped to the door. "I quit!" he barked. "I don't play with cheaters!"

"Cheaters! Look who's calling who a cheater. You're the cheater, you little brat!" Kelly shoved the game board across the table. It slid off and crashed to the floor, sending

a rainbow of pink and yellow and blue and green play
money into the air.

"I never wanted to play anyway," grumbled Ben, turning to go.

"You better help clean this mess up," called Kelly.

"You clean it. It's your room," yelled Ben as he disappeared down the hallway.

"You got the dumb game out!" cried Kelly. She sank
her aching head back on her pillow. She imagined Ben
changed into a frog, a huge, ugly frog, sitting on the chair
opposite her, playing Monopoly.

She grabbed her pen and her diary and wrote under
Wednesday, August 29:

> Ben is in big trouble. Anybody who cheats at Mo-
> nopoly deserves to be hexed. Ben is in for a terrible
> surprise. I hope he likes his frog, Fritzi. Because they
> are going to be very close friends.

The Witch's Spell

Kelly's hand shook as she rang Malvina Krebs' doorbell. She clutched a small paper bag in her left hand. Over a week had passed since the idea of casting a magic spell on Ben had entered her mind. All through her first day back at school, Kelly had thought about Ben and Malvina Krebs and witches and spells and hexes and frogs. And now here she was, standing on Malvina's front porch. The Thursday afternoon séance was over. The last car had just pulled out of Malvina's driveway.

The door creaked open. Malvina blinked her black eyes in the sunlight. She wore a baggy gray sweater and black slacks that were too short, exposing her bony ankles. "Marigold is over in the Gordens' yard, Kelly."

"I don't want Marigold, Mrs. Krebs. I'd like to talk to you, if you have a minute."

"To me?" Malvina's face brightened. "Come on in, dear, come right in. I'll get you some gingersnaps."

A strange chill ran through Kelly as she watched Malvina vanish into her kitchen. She glanced uneasily about the small living room as she sat down on one end of the sofa. The drapes were still pulled closed, giving the room a gloomy look even though it was only four thirty in the afternoon. Small blue candles still flickered in sconces that hung on the wall. Four other larger candles stood on tables. Shadows waved back and forth across the room. The largest candle of all burned brightly on the coffee table in front of Kelly. A ring of red berries and shiny leaves encircled the candle.

"Do you like gingersnaps?" asked Malvina, returning to the living room with a small blue china plate. Her mouth twisted into a tight little smile, but her eyes remained dark and questioning.

"Yes, thank you," said Kelly as she reached for a cookie. She didn't know what to say next.

"My séance went splendidly today," said Malvina, filling the silence. "We made contact with the spirits!" She placed the blue china plate on the end of the coffee table and sat down opposite Kelly. "We spoke with Leroy today, I'm sure of it!" Her small eyes sparkled in the candlelight.

"You did?" asked Kelly. Malvina's brother had died three years ago. Kelly wished now that she had brought Jennifer with her. She didn't like being all alone with someone as peculiar as Malvina Krebs.

"We closed our eyes," continued Malvina, "laid our hands on the coffee table, and called for the long-lost spirits, over and over. And then this table raised right up off the floor! I could feel it swaying under my hands, back and forth, back and forth, back and forth. The windows rattled as though they were hit by a gust of wind, and then

67

the ghosts floated into this very room! And Leroy, my dear departed brother, whispered into my ear, Kelly. Whispered right into my ear!" Malvina closed her eyes and leaned back in her chair.

"Are . . . are you sure someone in the room here wasn't talking, Mrs. Krebs? Or maybe someone lifted this table with their knees." Kelly tried to picture the coffee table floating in the air.

"It was Leroy," stated Malvina. She opened her eyes.

Kelly did not know what to think. Malvina Krebs was either a very special person with mysterious powers, or else she was crazy. "Mrs. Krebs," she spoke out suddenly, "do you have extraspecial powers?"

"Special powers?" questioned Malvina.

"Uh, what I mean is," stammered Kelly, "did you ever wish for something and make it happen?"

"My dear, I do that all the time." Malvina stared at Kelly.

"Do you have special powers to change things you don't like?" asked Kelly almost in a whisper. "I mean, could you . . . could you cast a spell on somebody?"

Malvina began to wring her hands and sway in her seat ever so slightly. "I did cast a spell once."

"When?" asked Kelly. She could feel her heart beating faster.

"Oh, it was on Roxanne Fisher, that girl down at Sweetley's Beauty Parlor. She ruined my hair one time. Just curled it up into a little ball of frizz. All I wanted was a wave." Malvina smiled her tight smile. "But I fixed her! All the way home, I kept saying 'I hope Roxanne Fisher's hair falls out, I hope Roxanne Fisher's hair falls out.' "

"Did it work?"

Malvina looked at Kelly and stopped wringing her hands. "Of course, it worked! The next time I saw Roxanne, she was wearing a blonde wig. And the time after that, she had a big beret on her head. It worked, all right."

"Could you cast a spell on Ben, Mrs. Krebs? Please?" Kelly said it so fast she could hardly believe her ears.

"On Ben? What has that boy done now?" asked Malvina.

"What hasn't he done! Marigold is so lucky, being an only child. She has her own room and her own toys. Ben is ruining my life. He pesters me, he punches me, he ducks me underwater in our pool, he cheats at Monopoly, and he gets into my things all the time. He's terrible, Mrs. Krebs. I wish I didn't have a brother. I wish he would just disappear!" Kelly twisted the top of the little brown bag that she had in her left hand.

"Your brother, Ben, I'm afraid, is a terror to the whole neighborhood," agreed Malvina. "Why, only the other day, he tore through my backyard on his bicycle, mind you, and knocked over two of my tomato plants and a row of beautiful zinnias."

"You never know where he'll pop up next," continued Kelly. "He's really a pest. I wish I could . . . Well, I wish I could make him disappear. Or turn him into a frog or something. Could you help me? Could you cast a spell on Ben with your special powers? Could you turn Ben into a frog? That would fix him!"

"A frog? Turn your brother into a frog? Do you really think I could?"

"He likes frogs so much. Let's make him one! It would serve him right. Maybe teach him a good lesson," said Kelly.

"I've never turned anyone into a frog. Nobody can do that!"

Kelly flushed pink with embarrassment. Suddenly the whole idea sounded absolutely ridiculous. "You're right," she said as she rose from the sofa. "It was a dumb idea." She started for the door.

"Wait a minute!" Malvina rubbed her chin with her long, skinny fingers. "Sit down. This idea is beginning to sound interesting."

"I wish I'd never thought of it," said Kelly, sitting back down.

"You know, I'd like to give it a try! Who knows? It just might work."

"Oh, come on," argued Kelly. "This really is crazy." But Malvina had a faraway look on her face, and Kelly knew it was too late to change her mind.

"Spells work better," said Malvina, "if you have something that belongs to the person."

"I have something. I've been reading about these things," answered Kelly. She opened her little brown bag and poured out several of Ben's fingernails on the coffee table. "His room is a horrible mess. I found these on his desk."

Malvina smiled her terrible smile, scooped up the fingernails, and said, "These will do nicely. Let's begin!" She gazed into the flickering flame of the candle and began to toss each fingernail into the fire as she chanted some words over and over.

Wind and rain and hail and fog,
If Ben is bad, make him a frog.

Malvina repeated her magical spell two more times as she threw Ben's fingernails into the flame. Kelly watched the orange sparks shoot upward. By the time Malvina had finished her chant, Kelly felt awful. What if something terrible really did happen to Ben? What if Malvina Krebs really *was* a witch?

Malvina suddenly stood up, craned her long neck toward the wall candles, and blew them out. Then she opened her curtains with one strong tug on the cord. Kelly saw Buster and Ben racing each other on their bicycles along the Hopper Street curb. All at once everything was normal again. Even Malvina Krebs looked normal.

Kelly stood up. "There's no way this spell can work."

"What?"

"Well, I mean, even if you are a wi— I mean, even if you do have special powers, nobody can change a boy into a frog."

"We shall see, dear, we shall see. My powers usually do not fail me." Her spidery form swept past Kelly to the front door. "But now I must go find Marigold. Goodness, it's almost dinnertime!" She opened the door and Kelly slipped out, happy to feel the warm sunshine again. She waved to Jennifer.

Jennifer ran down the sidewalk. She came up smiling and panting for breath. "Where've you been?" she demanded. "I wanted to study with you for that science test tomorrow."

Kelly felt her knees wobbling. "Jennifer, please! You've got to come with me to the hideout. Come on! I've got to ask you something." The two girls ran across the street and through the McCoys' back door. They crept single file along the basement ledge and tumbled into their hideout.

72

Kelly closed the doors and turned on the lamp. In the shadowy lamplight, she asked her question.

"Do you believe in ghosts and witches and things?"

Jennifer's brown eyes grew wide. "You bet I do!" she exclaimed. "The ghost of my great-great-uncle Zachary Jackson lives in our attic!"

"He does not," said Kelly, growing worried.

"He does too. I've heard him! He was the one who built our house years ago, and now he doesn't want to leave it. We still have his uniforms and pictures in a trunk in the attic. Every now and then, I'll wake up in the middle of the night and hear footsteps in the attic right over my bed!"

"Really?"

"Honest. It's Uncle Zachary's ghost! One night I even went up the steps to the attic, but then I got scared and ran back down."

"Well, how about witches? You don't believe in witches, do you?" asked Kelly.

"Witches I don't know about, only ghosts. But it's just eight more weeks 'til Halloween. Who knows? Maybe this Halloween, we'll see a real witch!"

"Maybe," said Kelly, chewing her thumbnail. She always chewed her thumbnail when she was worried, and now she was worried.

10

The Floating Test

The McCoys could usually look through their kitchen window and see clear across the Ohio River to the little houses dotting the blue hills of Kentucky. But Saturday, when they sat down for their pancake breakfast, all they could see was thick white mist rolling up from the river. Even the clump of trees that stretched out from the left corner of their yard was lost in a cloud of white.

"Guess who came to our school yesterday," said Ben. He speared a pancake with his fork.

"Who?" asked his mother and father together.

"A man from the Environmental Protection Agency. He said the Ohio River valley is one of the most polluted areas of the country. He said we should all pitch in to help clean it up."

Kelly poured syrup on her stack of pancakes. "We have air pollution, water pollution, people pollution, and every other kind of pollution," she added.

"Sounds awful," commented Dr. McCoy. He lifted the orange-juice pitcher.

"It *is* awful, Dad," said Ben. "And the worst thing is, all the fourth, fifth, and sixth graders have to write a report by next Wednesday."

"On what?" asked Mrs. McCoy.

"On the worst cause of pollution in Lawrenceburg. And I know what I'm writing about."

"What?" asked Kelly.

"About cigarette smokers. Dad, could I have one of your cigarettes to tape to the top of my report?" asked Ben.

Kelly's father groaned. "Do you have to? When are you going to leave me alone about smoking?"

"When you stop."

"Why don't you write about that Chihuahua down the street? It barks all day and half the night. Now, that's noise pollution."

"No, I'll stick with the cigarettes," said Ben. "Buster is writing about the Ohio River. He says it's full of oil and chemicals and junk. All those chemical companies upriver are polluting the water."

Kelly bit into a syrupy pancake. She felt better this morning. Two days had passed since her strange visit with Malvina Krebs. Early in the day, with her family all around her and the sun beginning to peep through the swirl of fog, things like witches and hexes didn't seem possible. She looked at Ben and sighed. He wasn't about to turn into a frog. Ben would stay Ben the rest of his life.

Ben looked up and caught Kelly's stare. He squinched

up his eyes, flapped out his ears with his hands, and stuck his tongue out as far as it would go.

"Mom, look!" said Kelly. She nodded toward Ben. Ben's face sprang back to normal.

"Mom," he said, "these pancakes of yours are the best in the whole world!" He smiled like an angel.

Dr. McCoy cleared his throat. "What are *you* writing about, Kelly? For your pollution report."

"I don't know, Dad. I should write about Ben. He sure ruins the environment."

"That's enough, Kelly!" said Mrs. McCoy. "Quit picking on your brother."

"But, Mom, it's people like Ben that cause pollution," explained Kelly. "I mean, what if everyone in Lawrenceburg kept their home as messy as Ben keeps his room? *And* he litters all over the street. Every time he gets a low grade, he throws his paper in the street on the way home from the bus stop."

"I only did that once!" argued Ben. "The time I got a D on my science test."

"You got a D?" asked Dr. McCoy, raising one eyebrow.

"And yesterday I even saw him spit, right on our driveway," added Kelly.

"Kelly!" exclaimed Mrs. McCoy.

"Well, he did, Mom. And he always wants to use that colored toilet paper. Gosh, everybody knows colored toilet paper adds dyes and stuff to the rivers."

"Kelly, I said that's enough! We're eating," scolded her mother.

"Well, he does," replied Kelly.

"I do not," yapped Ben.

"Yes, you do."

"No, I don't."

"Yes, you do."

"Kelly!" ordered Dr. McCoy. "Leave poor Ben alone! You're always yelling at him. No wonder he fights with you all the time."

Kelly looked down at her plate. There they go again, she thought. Always yelling at her. They never yell at Ben. Well, not enough, anyway.

Kelly's mother stood up and began to clear a few dishes from the table. "Monday I begin my new job," she announced. "Today we clean the house. I don't want to leave a dirty house."

"We?" questioned Dr. McCoy. "I'm working on the paneling in Kelly's new room. The carpet men are coming Tuesday."

"I have to work on my report, Mom," said Kelly. "That should take all day."

"I have to teach Fritzi how to jump," said Ben. "The pet contest at school is next week." Ben slithered out of his chair.

"Hold it!" Kelly's mother put her hands on her hips. "You're cleaning that dungeon of yours, Ben, from wall to wall. Samantha, you and Kelly clean up your room. Oh, and Kelly, I want you to help sort the laundry and put it away."

"Another Saturday ruined!" moaned Ben, dragging a dustcloth to his room.

A few minutes later, Kelly's mother dumped a large basketful of rumpled clothes onto the sofa. Kelly picked up her socks, twisted them together, and tossed them into

77

a pile. She listened to the sound of hammering coming from the basement and smiled. Soon her own private room would be ready.

She peered more closely at her white socks. Then she held up a T-shirt of Ben's and studied it. "Mom," she called. "What is this stuff?"

Her mother examined the little bits of gray fluff that were stuck to the clothes. She pulled some loose and sniffed it. "Ben!" she called. "Come here."

Ben bounded down the stairs.

"Do you have any idea what this fuzzy stuff is?" asked Mrs. McCoy.

Ben studied the white clothes. "Uh oh, I think I do," he said.

"What?"

"My mouse."

"Your mouse?" shrieked Kelly and her mother together.

"Don't worry, Mom. He was dead. I had him in my shirt pocket. I was going to bury him." Ben looked genuinely sorry for his mouse. "Do you think you could find his tail?" He lifted two of Samantha's undershirts. "I use them for bookmarks."

"Oh, Ben!" moaned Mrs. McCoy. "Not a mouse! What am I going to do with you?"

"I'm sorry, Mom."

"How many times have I told you to keep those dead things out of your pockets?"

"I'm never wearing these socks again, Mom," wailed Kelly. "Never!" She ran to the bathroom to wash her hands.

"It's really not such a big deal," yelled Ben after her.

"It's just a little fuzz on your stupid clothes. Gosh, you'd think you'd feel sorry for the poor mouse! How would you like to go round and round in a washing machine, huh?"

Kelly slammed the bathroom door as hard as she could.

Kelly kept a close eye on Ben all that day, watching for any change, but nothing unusual happened. Later that afternoon, after the housework was finished, she and Jennifer, Ben and Buster, and Samantha and Marigold kicked and splashed in the McCoys' pool. The temperature had risen to 88. The sun had burned away all the fog. Kelly's parents sat on the patio, sipping glasses of iced tea. Creepy chirped in his cage, which swung gently from the bottom branch of the old cherry tree. The children raced around and around inside the pool, trying to create a big whirlpool. Marigold tripped and fell facedown in the water and came up spluttering.

"Want me to teach you to swim, Marigold?" asked Kelly.

"My mother can teach me. She said she was coming over later," answered Marigold. "She wants to wear her new bathing suit."

Kelly grabbed Jennifer's arm and pulled her over to the side. "Did you hear that, Jennifer? Mrs. Krebs is coming!"

"So what?"

"Don't you see? This is our big chance! Now we can give her the floating witch test!" Kelly had already told Jennifer about her visit with Malvina Krebs and the terrible spell cast on Ben.

"Kelly!" Jennifer exclaimed. "You don't *really* think Mrs. Krebs is a witch, do you? She's not old enough to be a witch. And her hair is too short."

"I'm not sure," whispered Kelly, "but I'm going to find out."

"How?"

"Simple. My witchcraft book says that in Salem, Massachusetts, around three hundred years ago, they used to throw people into a lake to see if they were witches. If they floated, they were. If they sank, they weren't."

"Did anybody ever drown?" asked Jennifer.

"All the time," said Kelly. "But they figured at least if they drowned, they had proved to everyone that they weren't witches."

"Mrs. Krebs could *never* float," said Jennifer. "Only fat people float."

"Shhh!" Kelly put her finger to her lips. Malvina Krebs marched into the yard, carrying an orange beach towel. Her arms and legs looked like long white Popsicle sticks. Pumpkins stepped along behind her, his tail straight in the air.

"Do you mind if I take a little dip in your pool?" she asked Kelly's mother. "It's so dreadfully hot today!"

Mrs. McCoy stood up to get another iced tea. "Not at all, Malvina. I just may join you."

"The water's not too dirty, I hope?" Malvina squinted to see if the pool water was clear.

"I put chlorine in last night," muttered Dr. McCoy. He turned a magazine page.

"Mommy!" called Marigold. "Watch this! Look at me!" Marigold kicked up her feet and thrashed her arms about, moving a few feet through the water.

"Very good," called Malvina. She spread her towel across a chair, stepped to the pool, and climbed the ladder. "I didn't know you were such a good little swimmer,

Marigold." She watched her daughter and smiled her twisted smile.

Kelly suddenly threw herself on her back and spread her arms out. She tried to kick her feet to the surface, but they sank downward like two rocks. "I give up. I'll never learn how to float!" she shouted over the noise of the splashing children. "Can you float on your back, Mrs. Krebs?" She stood on her feet and waited.

"Float on my back? I earned a lifesaving badge when I was in high school." Malvina opened her mouth and breathed in deeply until her skinny cheeks filled up like a balloon. She slowly lay back on the water until her long nose and her two big toes pointed straight up to the sky. She floated like a canoe.

Later that evening, Dr. McCoy sat in his recliner and listened to a Mozart record. Samantha lined her pennies in a straight row on the floor. Ben knelt on his knees and poked at Fritzi, trying to make him jump. Kelly poured some birdseed into Creepy's cup. Malvina Krebs *must* be a witch, she thought. No one that thin can float unless . . . She glanced at Ben. He hadn't been too terrible today. Except, of course, when he let that miserable mouse go through the washer and dryer. That should have been bad enough to trigger any spell. No, thought Kelly, Ben would *never* turn into a frog. Malvina Krebs *couldn't* cast spells. That was ridiculous.

"I'm a good boy, I like Ben, I'm a good boy, I like Ben, I like Ben."

Kelly jerked her head toward Creepy. "Creepy can talk!" she yelled. "Listen!"

"I'm a good boy, I like Ben, I like Ben, I like Ben."

Ben stopped poking Fritzi and jumped up. "Hey, it worked! I taught Creepy how to talk!"

"*You* did?" Kelly looked from Creepy to Ben.

"Sure. It was easy. I put those words on the tape recorder and played it to him over and over when you weren't around."

"Ben, you had no business teaching Creepy those dumb sentences. He's my bird!"

"I'm a good boy, I like Ben, I like Ben, I like Ben," squawked Creepy. Kelly looked at her parakeet with disgust.

"You've got a real smart bird, Kelly," chuckled Ben.

All at once a shrill scream came from the kitchen. "Ben! Get this frog out of the kitchen sink. Hurry! I'm trying to wash the dishes here, for heaven's sake, not give your frog a bath." Ben ran to the sink and scooped up Fritzi along with a handful of soapsuds.

"Put him in his box this minute," ordered Mrs. McCoy.

"Aw, Mom, he's lonely in his box. Can't he stay out just a little longer?"

"Absolutely not! You keep that frog in his box, Ben, or you make a little cage for him outside in the garden where he belongs. I will not have that thing jumping in my dishwater!"

"Gosh, Mom, if it weren't for Fritzi, our house would be full of flies. Fritzi's tongue flicks out and catches bugs so fast you can't even see it."

"Well, it's nice to have a frog who does his share of the work around this house. But it's Fritzi's bedtime now, and yours too."

Kelly shuddered from head to toe as she thought of Malvina Krebs' magical words:

82

Wind and rain and hail and fog,
If Ben is bad, make him a frog.

If Malvina Krebs really was a witch, Fritzi would not be lonely much longer.

The People Pollution
Problem

On Monday afternoon, the yellow school bus roared to a
stop on the Hopper Street corner. The little flag that said
STOP popped out from the side of the bus. The long row
of cars behind came to a halt as the Hopper Street children
stepped down. Kelly jumped off and spotted the blue mailbox on the corner. She remembered the long white envelope that she had mailed Saturday, and she wondered if
the Greenwood Military Academy had received her letter.
She hoped enough postage was on the envelope and the
address was right.

Kelly and Jennifer walked along the sidewalk in the
warm afternoon sun and tried not to step on any cracks.
Slung across their backs were canvas backpacks filled with
spelling books, health books, and graded worksheets.
Kelly felt strange as she passed by her own house. The
front door was closed. The garage door was pulled down.
No one was home yet. Ben ran up the driveway.

"Wait!" she called. "We're supposed to go to Mrs. Tweel's today. Remember, Ben? Mom's at work."

"Oh, yeah," he answered. Ben bounded down past two houses to the Tweels' front porch.

It seemed funny, not going straight home. Samantha and Marigold were jumping rope on the Tweels' sidewalk. Kelly waved good-bye to Jennifer and joined Ben at the Tweels' front door.

"Come on in," said Mrs. Tweel with a smile on her broad face. "I've been waiting for you. Anybody hungry?"

"I am!" shouted Ben.

"Starved!" replied Kelly. They followed Mrs. Tweel to her kitchen and reached into a plate stacked with warm chocolate chip cookies. Ben took four cookies.

"Ben," said Kelly in a low voice. "Remember what Mom said about being a pig."

"Well, I'm hungry!" Ben popped a whole cookie into his mouth.

Tootles waddled in and sat down. Her jaw was going up and down as she tried to chew a big wad of pink bubble gum.

"I didn't know your poodle chewed gum," said Kelly.

"I'm afraid Tootles is very fond of bubble gum," answered Mrs. Tweel with a chuckle. "She goes outside and finds the stuff everywhere. I gave up a long time ago trying to break her of the habit." Tootles tossed her head from left to right as she chewed, trying to keep the gum from falling out of her mouth.

"Want a cookie, Tootles?" asked Mrs. Tweel. Tootles' tail wagged and she barked, dropping her chewing gum to the floor.

"Throw your gum away," ordered Mrs. Tweel. Tootles obediently picked up her gum, trotted to the wastebasket, dropped it in, and came back. She sat up on her hind legs and whined. Mrs. Tweel handed her a cookie.

"No wonder Tootles is so fat," laughed Kelly. "She looks like a big snowball."

Mrs. Tweel scratched behind Tootles' ear and gave her another cookie. "She's spoiled; yes, she is. Spoiled rotten little pup." Tootles barked and wagged her tail.

"Can I take Tootles for a walk, Mrs. Tweel?" asked Ben. He crammed one more cookie into his mouth.

"Would you like to go for a walk, Tootles?" asked Mrs. Tweel. Tootles' tail wagged even harder. "Let me get you her leash. And hold her tight. Don't let her get away." She and Ben and Tootles went to the garage to get the leash.

Kelly pulled out a kitchen chair and sat down. She glanced at the *Register* spread on the table. Her eye was caught by a picture of a house with a broken window. Under the picture were the words: *Vandalism—a growing problem in Lawrenceburg.*

"What's *vandalism?*" asked Kelly as Mrs. Tweel walked back into the kitchen.

"Vandalism?" Mrs. Tweel looked surprised. "Why, that's when bad people tear up and destroy other people's property just for the fun of it. Vandals smash windows and steal. They really do an awful lot of senseless damage." She pointed to the newspaper. "I was just reading about this house down on Hickory Street. Vandals hit it last Friday. I hope they catch the culprits."

"Who's doing it?"

"They don't know. But I'll tell you one thing—you'd

better lock your doors if you go anywhere. Who knows when they'll hit our street!" Mrs. Tweel picked up her sewing basket and walked into the dining room. Kelly followed her.

"I wish we had a watchdog," said Kelly. "Is Tootles a good watchdog?"

Mrs. Tweel laughed. "When she's not busy chewing gum, she is. She growls every now and then."

Kelly thought about her own home. She and Samantha and Ben kept a pretty sharp eye out for any strangers. They knew exactly who lived on Hopper Street and who didn't. "Say, Mrs. Tweel!" She snapped her fingers. "I've got a terrific idea!"

Mrs. Tweel spread a length of blue-and-red flowered cotton polyester on her dining-room table and opened an envelope full of dress pattern pieces. "What terrific idea?" she asked.

"I have the perfect solution to your problem!"

"What problem?" Mrs. Tweel looked up, confused.

"See, this man from the Environmental Protection Agency told us about people pollution. He said that someday there would be too many people and not enough food to feed them."

"Really?" asked Mrs. Tweel, still confused.

"Yes, and he said the average American family only has *two* children, Mrs. Tweel. Don't you see?"

"See what?" Mrs. Tweel put down her pattern pieces and listened harder.

"My parents have *three* children. They went over their quota! They're only supposed to have two. The best family is made up of one mother, one father, and two children. We have too many kids, see?"

"Hmmm." Mrs. Tweel wrinkled her forehead. "I still don't see what that has to do with *my* problem. What *is* my problem, anyway?"

"Don't you get it? You and poor Mr. Tweel are stuck here in this huge house with no children, not even one. And with you such a great chocolate chip cookie baker! And then there's my family cramped into our little house with so many kids my mom had to go and get a job just to get away from all the racket. It's not fair, don't you see? We'll give you Ben! That way we'll have two children, and you and Mr. Tweel will at least have one. Doesn't that sound good?"

Kelly was excited. This plan was so simple! Why hadn't she thought of this before? It would make everyone happy. Her father could listen to his records without so much noise. Her mother wouldn't have to worry about mice in the washing machine. The Tweels would finally have a little boy of their own. Tootles would get a playmate. And Ben would become an only child. Everyone knew how many cookies and new clothes and new toys an only child got. But best of all, thought Kelly with a tremble of delight, I'd be rid of Ben for good.

"What do you think, Mrs. Tweel? Wouldn't you love to have Ben? You'd never have to worry about robbers or vandals or anything. Ben has real sharp eyes. Between Ben and Tootles, your house will be well protected!" Kelly smiled.

"A perfect family, Kelly, is not necessarily one mother, one father, and two children." Mrs. Tweel sat down and drew Kelly to her. Kelly leaned against the chair. "A perfect family comes in all different shapes and sizes. Some families are big and some are small. The family's size is not what counts. It's how well it fits together. It's something like a jigsaw puzzle."

"A jigsaw puzzle?"

"You know when you lose a piece to your jigsaw puzzle, it just doesn't look quite right, does it? If you lost one person in your family, your family wouldn't seem quite right either."

"Our family would be fine without Ben! His room is a mess, he forgets to put his dirty socks in the hamper, and he even forgets to drain the bath water from the bathtub. My mother can't stand him!"

"Now, Kelly," sighed Mrs. Tweel. "She may hate the things he does sometimes, but I'm sure she loves Ben. She would never give Ben to me! In fact, I wouldn't even *want* him."

"You wouldn't want Ben?" asked Kelly, surprised. She was sorry she had mentioned his dirty socks. "But Ben is a bargain! Just think, for absolutely nothing, you would get a smart little boy who could take Tootles for a walk every day, cut your grass, wash dishes, and clean windows. Ben can do practically anything."

"But I have enough dirty socks to wash," protested Mrs. Tweel.

"Forget the dirty socks! With only one child to care for, you could teach Ben to take better care of his room. He needs you, Mrs. Tweel!"

Mrs. Tweel laughed. "Oh, I like Ben. It's just that Mr. Tweel and I don't . . . Well, we don't really want any children."

Kelly was shocked. "You don't like children?"

"Oh, we like children. We love children! Other people's children. But we don't want any of our own."

"You don't?" Kelly was stunned. "I thought everyone wanted children."

"Not everyone. Mr. Tweel and I like to travel. It's hard to travel with kids."

"You don't want Ben, do you?"

"You'd better keep him. He's *your* brother."

"I'll come and wash your windows every Saturday morning if you'll take him," pleaded Kelly.

"No, thanks." Mrs. Tweel laughed. "He's all yours."

"But I don't want him! I don't want him!" cried Kelly. She slammed her hand down on the dining-room table. "*Nobody* wants Ben. I can't even give him away."

"One of these days you'll be glad you have a brother," said Mrs. Tweel. She picked up her scissors and smoothed her red-and-blue flowered material.

"Never!" exclaimed Kelly. "I never asked for him. How come *I* got stuck with him?"

Mrs. Tweel looked straight at Kelly. "Life would be a whole lot easier for you if you just tried to get along with him. I bet he'd be shocked. Ever try it?"

"Are you kidding? No one could get along with that brat. He's a real pain." Kelly stomped to the front door and spun around. Her green eyes glistened with tears.

"Is it five o'clock yet?"

Mrs. Tweel glanced at the clock on the wall. "Four thirty."

"I think I'll take a walk, OK?"

"All right, Kelly. But stay on this block."

"I will." Kelly ran outside and down the Tweels' side-walk. She stopped suddenly and caught her breath. Pulling into the McCoys' driveway was a dark green car that Kelly had never seen before. She walked to her yard as the car came to a stop in her driveway. On the side of the car were the words *Greenwood Military Academy*.

A tall man opened the car door and stepped out. He carried a black briefcase. Kelly felt her heart beat faster. They got my letter! she thought. They've come to get Ben!

A Military Maneuver

Kelly rushed up her front sidewalk just as the tall man in the dark blue suit reached for the doorbell. "Uh, can I help you?" she spluttered. "I live here. My name's Kelly—Kelly McCoy."

The tall man dropped his hand from the doorbell and peered at Kelly over the top of his glasses. "Kelly McCoy? You must be Ben McCoy's sister."

"I am," stated Kelly. She glanced at Ben, who was walking down the sidewalk with Tootles jumping and pulling at the leash. "Ben's not home. But he should be back any minute."

"I'm Mr. Marchman, assistant director of Greenwood Military Academy." He looked at his gold watch. "We received your brother's application for our school today, but he failed to fully complete the form."

"He did?" asked Kelly, trying hard to look surprised.

"I live quite near you and decided to talk with Ben myself and complete his application. Today is the last day

92

to register." Mr. Marchman looked at his watch again and frowned. "You say he's not home?"

"He's . . . he's at work."

"Oh? What does he do?"

"He works with animals. Dogs and things like that," answered Kelly. Mr. Marchman sat down on the porch glider and snapped open his briefcase. He whipped out Kelly's long white envelope and unfolded the application form.

"Your brother forgot to fill in his age," stated Mr. Marchman, clicking the end of his ball-point pen. "What is Ben's age?"

"Gosh, Ben's age. Hmmm, let's see now." Kelly looked up at a puffy cloud and began to count her fingertips. "His birthdays roll around so fast, I'm not really sure anymore. You'd never believe he's as old as he is, though. Ben's been very sick. He looks a lot smaller than most boys his age," she said.

"He *must* be in good physical condition. That's a requirement," said Mr. Marchman, shaking his head. "Greenwood Military Academy has an extremely strenuous schedule. Our students are not mollycoddled. They have got to measure up, work hard, toe the line. Our school is not for just anybody. We believe in strict discipline and high academic achievement."

"Strict discipline! Good! That's just what Ben needs. My parents are too easy on him, way too easy. Greenwood Military Academy will be perfect for Ben, just perfect." Kelly sighed with satisfaction.

"I'm afraid too many of our students were once behavior problems but, believe me, Greenwood Military Academy straightens them out fast. We tolerate absolutely no monkey business," said Mr. Marchman with a note of pride. He fidgeted with his pen and pushed his glasses higher on his nose.

"It'll be good for Ben," said Kelly. "He needs a lot of straightening out."

"What are Ben's future plans? Do you know what career your brother is interested in?"

"What he wants to be?" asked Kelly. "Sure. Ben wants to be a chemist. He likes mixing and stirring things around in pots."

"Has he thought of his future military plans? Most of our graduates do go on to military careers, you know."

"You mean like soldiers and airplane pilots?"

"Exactly. We offer a broad curriculum at Greenwood, but we stress a military career."

"You mean Ben would have to fight in a war?"

"It is a possibility if he pursues a military career."

Kelly remembered seeing pictures of soldiers shooting and killing on the six o'clock news. She wasn't sure she wanted Ben to become a soldier. Out of the corner of her eye, she saw Ben throwing a stick to Tootles in the Tweels' front yard. Tootles scampered about as Ben yelled, "Fetch!"

"I don't know." Kelly grabbed both her elbows as she felt a sudden chill. "I don't know if I want Ben to become a soldier. He's my only brother. I wouldn't want him to get killed in a war."

Mr. Marchman drummed his fingers impatiently on the side of the black briefcase. "To defend your country, young lady, is an honor. Somebody has to do it."

"I know. I know. But I don't want it to be Ben. He's the only brother I have."

Mr. Marchman shrugged his shoulders. "It's not for you to decide, is it? Your brother has already decided."

Kelly suddenly wanted to get rid of this man on her front porch. She thought fast. "But . . . poor Ben. He was so very sick!"

"Ah yes, that illness you mentioned. Just when was he so sick and what was the nature of his illness?" asked Mr. Marchman, readying his pen over the application form.

"It was terrible! It happened right after he worked as a counselor at Camp Wiggy Wammy."

"Oh?"

"At first they thought it was poison ivy, but it wasn't."

"What was it?" asked Mr. Marchman, readying his pen.

"The creeping fungus."

"The what?"

"The creeping fungus," repeated Kelly, looking straight at Mr. Marchman. "You've never heard of it? It's sort of like the black plague, but instead of turning black, you break out with hideous pink splotches all over your body. Oh, they gave Ben medicine, but that just made his skin look like crusty old mud."

"It did?"

"I tell you, Ben was a mess. We thought he was going to die!" Mr. Marchman leaned forward and scribbled as fast as he could on his paper. "The doctors had given him up for lost," she continued. "They even stopped coming to the house after a while. You see, Ben was highly contagious. Some say he still is."

"I think this is a joke!" said Mr. Marchman. "The creeping fungus?"

"Of course! Really, I'm surprised you've never heard of it. I thought everyone had heard by now."

"You say it's contagious?"

"Oh, don't worry. Ben's in the final stages. He glows in the dark now. That's a sure sign that the contagious period is past. I think."

"You must be joking."

"This is no joking matter! If it lasts 'til Halloween, he won't need a costume. We even had a sign on our front door for months. It said:

QUARANTINE
CREEPING FUNGUS
HIGHLY CONTAGIOUS

"We just took it down this morning. Would you like to see it?"

"No, no! That won't be necessary." Mr. Marchman clicked his pen, stuffed the application into his briefcase, snapped it shut, and stood up.

"The really awful thing is, though, what it did to poor Ben." Kelly tried hard to bring tears to her eyes but couldn't do it.

"What else did it do to him?"

"Well, here he is starting the ninth grade, and he looks just like a fourth grader. He shrunk up! He used to be so strong and tall, and now he's a puny little pipsqueak."

"I don't believe it! This *must* be a prank." Mr. Marchman started for the porch steps.

"A prank?" Kelly sounded hurt. "Why do you think Ben *wants* to go to Greenwood Academy? He thought a good military school would build him back up again—make a man of him."

"I'm very sorry, young lady. But I don't think your brother is right for our school. In fact, our classes are already filled." Mr. Marchman strode down the steps and hurried to his car.

Ben raced across the front yard with Tootles pulling at the leash. "Kelly!" he yelled. "Help me give this dog a bath. He's been digging in the garden again, looking for bones." Ben accidentally bumped into Mr. Marchman. "Whoops, sorry." He studied Mr. Marchman from head to foot.

Mr. Marchman jumped in his car and slammed the door. "You're not Ben McCoy, are you?"

"That's me! Glad to meet you." Ben thrust his mud-covered hand through the open car window. Mr. Marchman stared at Ben's hand, turned on the ignition, and screeched out of the McCoy driveway.

"Gee, what a grouch!" said Ben.

"No one shakes hands with you, Ben," laughed Kelly. "Look at your hands. They're covered with mud."

"I can't help that. I was helping Tootles dig for bones. Help me give her a bath, come on," he begged.

A small yellow car rolled down Hopper Street. The horn gave two little honks. "Here comes Mom!" hollered Kelly. "Sorry, I have to feed Creepy and give *him* a bath. Thursday is the big pet show."

"That bird won't win anything," teased Ben as he ran back down the driveway.

Kelly watched Ben leave. She could have always changed a frog back into Ben if she wanted. But if he went to war and was killed, she could never change that back.

13

The Great Escape

Kelly awakened with a sudden cry. She sat upright in bed and listened. She could still hear her scream in the quiet bedroom. Samantha rolled over beside her.

What a nightmare! She and Ben were soldiers, and they were running across bridges and over mountains. Hundreds of enemy soldiers chased them. They shot at them with guns. Ben fell on a sharp rock. He called for Kelly to help. It was a terrible dream.

Kelly slipped her feet into her fluffy bedroom slippers, picked up her diary, and tiptoed in the dark to the kitchen. She turned on the ceiling light and wrote under Tuesday, September 11:

> Ben is a brat but he is my brother. I really don't want anything terrible to ever happen to him. He's the only brother I have. Maybe Mrs. Tweel is right. Our family would seem strange without him. I'm glad I got rid of that awful man from the Greenwood Military Academy.

That afternoon after school, Kelly broke off bits of lettuce into salad bowls and carefully sliced three tomatoes and seven radishes.

"I put the chocolate pudding in the refrigerator to cool, Mom."

"Thanks. You're a real help. You don't know how tired I am. And I still have to mop the floor. My shoes are sticking to it."

"That's the orange juice I spilled this morning. I'll mop it after dinner."

"Thanks, Kelly." Mrs. McCoy walked to the front door and poked her head outside. "Ben! Samantha! Dinnertime!" In a few minutes, the family gathered around the table. All except Ben.

"Where's Ben?" asked Dr. McCoy.

"He was just in the backyard a few minutes ago," answered Kelly's mother. At that moment, a heavy pounding sounded on the back door. Kelly and Samantha popped up out of their chairs and raced to open it. Kelly won. She threw open the door.

"Come quick! Ben's hung himself! Hurry!" Buster shouted. His eyes popped out of his chubby face.

Dr. and Mrs. McCoy rushed to the back door. Everyone pushed and tumbled into the yard.

"Where is he? Where is he?" screamed Mrs. McCoy.

"Over there!" shouted Buster, pointing to the cherry tree.

Ben's foot was caught in a tangle of rope that twisted and looped from branch to branch of the cherry tree, then stretched clear across ten feet of space to the gutter along the McCoys' roof. It was attached to the gutter by a huge plastic hook. Ben dangled upside down, waving his arms

and screaming. His kicking pulled the rope tighter around his ankle. "Help! Don't just stand there! Get me out of this mess!"

Everyone rushed to help at once. They untangled the rope and lowered a red-faced Ben to the ground.

"My clothesline! You took my good clothesline!" cried Mrs. McCoy.

"My gutter!" exclaimed Kelly's father, eyeing the drooping gutter, which was torn loose from the side of the house. "Benjamin Harris McCoy, you are in *big trouble*, very big trouble." Dr. McCoy ran his hands through his hair and groaned. "What are you trying to do, pull the whole house down?"

"Doesn't anyone care about me?" cried Ben. "I almost killed myself!"

"You could try being more careful," said Dr. McCoy.

"I couldn't help it, Dad," protested Ben. "I was Spiderman, see. We built this great big spiderweb out of rope, and I was trying to swing from the cherry tree to the roof. When Spiderman does it, it looks easy." Ben rubbed his sore ankle.

Samantha ran to the cherry tree and tried to climb up the trunk. "Get down," ordered Dr. McCoy. "We'll have no more Spiderman stunts today."

"You're not allowed to get on the roof, Ben," scolded Mrs. McCoy. "Don't you *ever* do that again. You could fall and break your neck!"

"He had to get on the roof," shouted Buster. Everyone looked at Buster except Ben. Ben squinched his eyes closed and covered his ears with his hands. Buster's face turned bright red. "He . . . he had to get on the roof," he stammered, "to get Kelly's parakeet."

"My parakeet?" screamed Kelly. "Oh, no, not Creepy!" She strained her eyes to see along the length of the roof. She couldn't find Creepy. "Ben!" she cried. "I ought to tar and feather you. I ought to . . ."

"Take it easy," said Kelly's mother. "Ben is really going to get it for this little trick."

"Gosh, Mom, I couldn't help it!" protested Ben. "Why do you always blame me for everything? If Kelly would ever exercise her bird, I wouldn't have let him out of his cage, and none of this would have happened."

"Blame it on me, why don't you! How *did* Creepy get outside?" demanded Kelly.

"Well . . . I opened his cage and let him out just so he could play on my head. You know how he likes to pick at the hair on the top of your head," explained Ben.

"I know, I know," said Kelly. She glared at her brother with her hands on her hips.

"Well," continued Ben, "Buster knocked on the door, and I opened it. I didn't know Creepy would fly right off my head. But he did. That dumb bird took off like a rocket before we could slam the door closed."

"Oh no!" wailed Kelly. The pet show was only two days away. She tried hard to fight back her tears.

"Wow! You should have seen him," added Buster. "He flew around and around the cherry tree like my toy airplane on the end of its string. We tried to catch him, but he was too fast."

"One time he landed on the picnic table, and I reached out my finger to him," said Ben, "but he flew up to the roof."

"He'll die," moaned Kelly. "Creepy's not used to the big wild outdoors. He won't know how to take care of himself. He's going to die!" She stood up and began to walk around the house, keeping her eyes glued to the roof.

"There he is! I see him! I see him!" cried Samantha. She jumped up and down and pointed to the gutter. Sure enough, Creepy had fluttered over to the gutter and was perched on the edge.

"Here, Creepy, come here, boy, pretty bird, pretty bird," sang Kelly. Buster tried to whistle.

"Look!" exclaimed Kelly. She had spotted Malvina Krebs' cat. Pumpkins crept into the yard like a tiny tiger on the prowl. He suddenly stopped and tilted his head upward. His narrow green eyes focused on Creepy.

"Dad, help me get the ladder. Please!" cried Kelly. Kelly and her father raced to the garage and lugged back the ladder. They leaned it against the side of the house.

"I'll go up," said Kelly. "I have to, Dad. I'm the only one Creepy will come to. He'll just fly away from you."

"Hurry!" said Dr. McCoy.

"Be careful, Kelly," warned her mother. Samantha and Ben tried to shoo Pumpkins away. But the orange cat zipped up the cherry tree and slunk along a branch, placing one padded foot carefully in front of the other.

"Hurry!" screamed Samantha.

Kelly clambered onto the white shingles and put her finger to her lips. "Shhh!"

Everyone got quiet except Samantha, who kept hopping about and shouting, "There goes Pumpkins! He's going to jump!" The cat jumped from the branch to the corner of the roof. He crouched low, never once taking his eyes off the little blue parakeet. His tail flicked left and right as he waited for just the right moment to pounce.

Kelly carefully stepped across the roof and then stopped

three feet from Creepy. "Here Creepy, here birdie, birdie, birdie." She held out her finger and inched closer.

Pumpkins moved forward. His furry body almost slid along the roof. His green eyes never blinked.

"Here Creepy, here boy," coaxed Kelly. She kneeled on the roof and reached for Creepy, slowly cupping her right hand around the tired little bird. Pumpkins leaped, but Kelly stood up holding Creepy gently in her hand. The cat's claws dug into the shingles by Kelly's feet, and then he darted away.

"I got him!" she called. Kelly climbed down the ladder and brought Creepy safely back inside the kitchen.

"No television for two weeks, Ben," said Dr. McCoy, following Ben and Kelly into the kitchen.

"No television! What did *I* do?" complained Ben.

"What did you do? You took your mother's clothesline. You ruined my gutter. You almost lost your sister's pet bird. You could have killed yourself with that silly rope trick and now . . . now our dinner is cold! No TV for two weeks, do you hear?"

Ben stomped upstairs to his room and slammed the door.

Later that evening, Kelly brushed her teeth and put on her long pink-and-white nightgown. She climbed into bed and reached for her diary. It was gone! She searched her room and ran downstairs to search the family room and kitchen.

"Kelly, it's past your bedtime. No more stalling," said her father.

"But I can't find my diary. It just disappeared! I had it this morning. I think you-know-who hid it."

"Ben?"

"Of course. Who else would steal my diary?" said Kelly.

"Don't accuse anyone until you're sure. Now get in bed."

"But he'll read it! I've got my most secret thoughts in that book!" Kelly flew upstairs and yanked open Ben's door. "Give me back my diary! You took it!"

"Get outta my room." Ben hurled his pillow at Kelly and hit her smack in the face.

Missing!

The next day, after dinner, Kelly helped her father carry a bright green carpet down the basement steps and over to her new bedroom. They pushed and pulled and cut off strips of carpeting here and there until the carpet fit just right.

"Like it?" asked Kelly's father, looking pleased.

"I sure do! Can I sleep here tonight?" asked Kelly.

"We haven't got the furniture in yet."

"That's OK. I'll just bring down my sleeping bag and my alarm clock." Kelly ran upstairs to gather a few things for her big move.

"Kelly!" called Mrs. McCoy. "Don't you think the birdcage needs cleaning? You're not taking it to school tomorrow looking like this, I hope."

"Gosh, you're right. I almost forgot." Kelly rushed off to the kitchen cabinet to get a clean sheet of gravel paper for Creepy's cage and some birdseed.

"My favorite show is coming on now," said Ben. He sat in front of the television set in the family room and looked glum. "Can't we start my punishment tomorrow night? I don't want to miss 'Star Ships.' Please, Mom?"

"No TV for two weeks. No use crying about it."

Grumbling to himself, Ben flipped open his box of pens. He wrote on one sheet of paper after another with the pen filled with invisible ink. After a few minutes, he gathered all his papers and the box of pens under his arm and stomped upstairs to his room.

"Mom, guess what!" yelled Kelly. "We're out of gravel paper! I've got to have some. What a time to run out."

Kelly's father clumped up the basement stairs. "Let's run over to Murphy's Mart," he suggested. "I need to buy some edging for that carpet."

"Samantha!" called Kelly's mother. "Get your jacket on. We're going down to Murphy's Mart for a few minutes."

"Right this minute?" asked Samantha.

"Right this minute," answered Mrs. McCoy as she walked into the family room. "Ben!" she called.

"I'm staying here," grumbled Ben, coming to the top of the stairs.

"Come on with us, Ben."

"I have to study my spelling. I don't want to go."

"It's all right. He can stay," said Kelly's father. "We'll be back in a few minutes." He turned to go. "Oh, and remember," he called over his shoulder, "no TV."

The McCoys had a flat tire on the way home and didn't pull into the garage until after dark. "Ben?" called Mrs. McCoy as she opened the kitchen door. Something was wrong. The whole house was dark. And it was too quiet. Dr. McCoy switched on the kitchen light.

"Ben? Ben?" he hollered.

"The television's gone!" exclaimed Mrs. McCoy. "Stan, where's the TV? Where's Ben?"

Kelly spotted her birdcage in the corner of the family room. "Look! Even Creepy is gone!"

"Ben!" shouted Dr. McCoy, rushing to the basement.

"Ben!" hollered Kelly's mother. She ran upstairs and searched each bedroom.

"It's those vandals, Dad," said Kelly as her father came huffing and puffing up the basement stairs with a distressed look on his face.

"You mean those hoodlums that hit Hickory Street?"

"I bet it is, Dad. They took a TV there, too."

"But they wouldn't take a little boy, would they? Ben!"

"Do you think Ben ran away and took the TV with him?" asked Samantha.

"Ben couldn't carry the television set. They probably came in through the back door and then took Ben so he couldn't identify them," said Kelly's father.

Mrs. McCoy hurried back down the stairs. "Ben has been kidnapped?"

"We'll find him, now, we'll find him."

"Kidnapped!" Kelly's mother covered her face with her hands.

Dr. McCoy called the police. Five minutes later, a black-and-white police car with a flashing red light rolled into the McCoys' driveway, and Sergeant Sinclair knocked on the door.

"Our son is missing," reported Dr. McCoy, "and our

house has been burglarized. The only thing taken, though, is the TV set."

"And my parakeet," added Kelly.

Sergeant Sinclair wrote some lines in a little black notebook as he walked from one room to another. Everyone followed him upstairs. "Which room is your son's?" he finally asked.

Mrs. McCoy pointed across the hall. The policeman looked inside and searched the room with his keen eyes. "This place sure has been ransacked," he said, jotting down a few notes.

"No, no, officer. This room hasn't been touched. It always looks like this, I'm afraid," said Mrs. McCoy.

"Where's Ben's toy rifle?" asked Kelly. She pointed to the wall. "It's gone!"

"That's right." Mrs. McCoy looked puzzled. "I wonder what that could mean?"

Kelly peeked into Fritzi's cardboard box. The frog sat in his saucer of water and blinked his black eyes. Kelly ran into her bedroom and threw herself across the bed. Ben was all alone with robbers, she thought. She spotted some pieces of paper on the heater duct on the floor. The invisible-ink words on the paper had turned blue in the heat. She quickly read:

KELLY SNOOPS IN MY ROOM.

She picked up another piece of paper and held it over the heater.

*MOM AND DAD LOVE
KELLY AND SAMANTHA.
EVERYBODY HATES ME.*

She picked up a third piece of paper, heated it, and read:

KELLY GETS A NEW ROOM.
SHE GETS EVERYTHING
JUST BECAUSE SHE'S OLDER.
I DON'T GET ANYTHING.

Kelly frowned as she studied the papers. Could it be that Ben hated her as much as she hated him? She ripped off a sheet of blank paper that was taped to her mirror. She held it over the heater and read:

NOBODY LIKES ME. NOBODY WANTS ME.
I CAN'T EVEN WATCH TV.
I'M RUNNING AWAY. YOU WILL BE SORRY.
GOOD-BYE,
BEN

P.S. DON'T BOTHER LOOKING.
YOU WILL NEVER FIND ME.

"Mom! Dad!" screamed Kelly as she dashed downstairs and into the family room. She waved the notes over her head. "Look at this. Ben ran away!"

Everyone, even Sergeant Sinclair, leaned over Kelly's shoulder and studied the papers. "Could it be," asked Dr. McCoy, "that Ben left right after we did? And then later burglars broke in and stole the television set while no one was home?"

Sergeant Sinclair checked the doors. "The back door is unlocked. Your theory is probably right."

"You mean Ben is outside right now in the dark with dangerous hoodlums prowling around?" cried Mrs. McCoy. Her voice began to shake.

111

"What are we standing here for?" shouted Kelly. "Let's go look for him. We're not going to leave him outside all night, are we?"

"Maybe Ben went swimming in the pool," suggested Samantha.

"The pool!" shrieked Kelly's mother. Everyone raced to the backyard. Sergeant Sinclair brought a spotlight from his car and switched it on. The McCoys' backyard lit up.

"He's not in the pool," said Dr. McCoy. "Let's search the woods. Come on. Ben!" he yelled over and over. "Ben! Ben!"

"Ben, where are you?" shouted Mrs. McCoy.

"Ben!" called Kelly. She was surprised at how worried she was. Her hands were shaking and her legs felt weak. She had always wanted to be rid of Ben, but now that he *was* gone, she felt horrible. What if something terrible happened to him? It would be all her fault.

A hand suddenly gripped Kelly's shoulder. "What's all this about Ben?" asked Malvina. She clutched her sweater tightly with her left hand as a chill wind began to blow.

"We can't find him," answered Kelly.

"I wanna go home!" cried Marigold. She pulled at Malvina's sleeve.

"Croak!" A huge spotted frog jumped out of the bushes into the glaring spotlight and landed on Malvina's shoe. It blinked its bulgy eyes at her and croaked again.

"Ben?" shrieked Malvina. Marigold screamed and jumped back.

The frog hopped two feet away and then leaped again. It had almost reached the shadows when Kelly sprang forward and grabbed it with both hands. She held the frog up in front of Malvina's nose.

"Please tell me this isn't Ben. Please!"

"It's not! It's not!" cried Malvina. She looked around and then quickly whispered into Kelly's ear, "I don't know a thing about casting spells. Not a thing. Absolutely nothing!"

"I don't want Ben to *ever* look like this. He's not that bad!"

"Of course he's not. Of course!" Malvina swatted at the frog. "Get that ugly thing away from me."

Kelly ran to the garage and found a plastic pail. She dropped the spotted frog in and laid a piece of cardboard across the top. Jennifer and her parents hurried across the street. Buster popped his head out of his front door. "What's the matter?" he called. "What's the police car doing in your driveway?"

"Ben," cried Kelly. "He's missing."

Soon the Gordens, the Jacksons, the Tweels, and a dozen other neighbors wandered all around the front yards and backyards with flashlights, lighting up every bush and tree.

"Find Ben, Tootles, find Ben!" coaxed Mrs. Tweel. Tootles barked and began to tear around and around the McCoys' backyard. Pumpkins crouched in the top of the cherry tree and watched, his orange fur raised straight up along his back.

"Oh, my good buddy Ben. My good buddy Ben," wailed Buster. He peered over the side of the swimming pool.

"He might die out here!" said Jennifer in her most dramatic voice. "Wild animals roam these woods at night."

"And robbers, too," piped up Samantha.

"Be quiet, you two," said Kelly. A few leaves drifted

down from the trees. A large, billowy gray cloud covered the moon and stars, making the night even darker.

Malvina Krebs ran back and forth by the edge of the woods, wringing her hands. She suddenly grabbed Mrs. McCoy's arm. "Have you checked in his bed?" she screeched. "Are you sure he's not sleeping in his bed?"

"Ben is gone, Malvina. He's gone!"

Malvina grasped her head with both hands, closed her eyes, and sighed loudly. Mrs. McCoy hurried away. "Oh my, oh my," Malvina wailed, "what have I done? What have I done?"

"My good buddy Ben," sobbed Buster. "And tomorrow we were going to play in our tepee!"

"What tepee?" asked Kelly.

"We just made a tepee today. Out in the woods at the end of our Indian trail."

"Buster!" yelled Kelly. "Show me your tepee!"

Buster, Jennifer, and Kelly felt their way carefully along the path in the woods. Buster led the way with his flashlight. Sticks broke under their feet and branches snapped back in their faces, but finally they came to three clothesline poles propped up and tied together. They lifted the flap of the old sheet that was draped over the poles and peeked inside.

There lay Ben, stretched out and sound asleep with his arm over his toy rifle. Buster's flashlight lit up a book on first aid for camping trips and a small suitcase.

"Wake up, Ben," Kelly and Jennifer cried together. Buster flashed the light onto Ben's face. Ben blinked his eyes and then scrambled to his knees.

"Everyone is out looking for you, Ben," said Kelly. "You'd better come home right now!"

A half hour later, after all the neighbors had returned home and Sergeant Sinclair had left with a promise to find the burglars and the television set, Kelly slipped some fresh gravel paper into her empty birdcage. "I don't know why those crooks had to take my little Creepy," she said. "It's bad enough they stole the TV."

"We've got Ben home," said her father. "That's the important thing." He gave Ben a big squeeze and tousled his haystack hair. "It is strange about Creepy, though. Very strange."

Mrs. McCoy stood in front of Ben and pointed her finger at him. "I'll tell you one thing, young man. You gave me the scare of my life! You pull that little running-away stunt again and you'll be in *big* trouble with me, real big trouble! Do you hear?" Ben scrunched down deeper into his chair.

Kelly turned away and chuckled. She didn't need to plot a way to get rid of Ben. She didn't need to arrange trouble in his life. He was doing a fine job of getting in trouble all by himself. Poor Ben! She almost felt sorry for him.

Kelly glanced up and saw Ben looking at her. "Sorry you lost your bird," he said. "You want me to help you look for him?"

"No, that's OK. Creepy is gone," answered Kelly. "This time he's gone for good." She suddenly felt strange, almost guilty. After all, she had wished Ben gone, out of her family, out of her life. And now here he was offering to help her find Creepy.

She looked straight at Ben. "I'm really glad it's Creepy who is missing and not you." Ben grinned.

116

"Nobody took Creepy," said Samantha in a very small voice.

"What?"

"Nobody took Creepy. I let him out of his cage right before we left for the store." Samantha started to cry. "I only wanted to play with him."

"Oh, Samantha! Not you, too?" said Kelly.

"He flew away that way," said Samantha. She pointed toward the stairs. "I was afraid to tell you. I knew you'd be mad."

"We can find him!" said Ben, jumping up from the chair. Samantha looked behind the bookcase. Mrs. McCoy looked in the kitchen.

After several minutes, Ben ran back into the family room. "I got him!" he said, holding Creepy in his upraised fist. Kelly opened the birdcage door and Creepy fluttered to his perch, squawking and scolding.

"And look what else I found," said Ben, holding up Kelly's diary. "It was behind your bed table. Creepy was pecking at it." He handed the diary to Kelly. "I told you I didn't take it. Why would I want to read your dumb old diary?" He yawned.

"Bedtime," announced Mrs. McCoy. "If nobody else is going to bed, I am. I'm exhausted!"

"Are we going to get our TV back?" asked Samantha, dragging her ragged blanket to her bed.

"I hope so." Mrs. McCoy kissed Samantha on the forehead. "Sergeant Sinclair will call us tomorrow."

Kelly slipped out to the garage, picked up the pail with the spotted frog, and hurried back to Ben's bedroom.

"Girls aren't allowed," Ben said sleepily.

"I got you something," whispered Kelly. She dumped the huge frog into Fritzi's cardboard box. "A friend for Fritzi."

"Really?" Ben hopped out of bed and looked into the box. "Hey, thanks! Fritzi's been needing a good friend. Now he won't be so lonely."

"I know," said Kelly. "Let's fix them a little cage in the garden tomorrow. You want to?"

"I want to! And then maybe we could—"

"Into bed!" bellowed Kelly's father, "before I count to three. One . . . two . . ."

Kelly darted out of Ben's room and bounded down the basement steps to her new bedroom. She curled into her warm sleeping bag and called out, "Leave the stairway light on. It's dark down here!"

About the Author

LINDA GONDOSCH received her Master's in English from North Kentucky University. She has four children who inspired her to start writing for children. Her books are based loosely on her family and town of Lawrenceburg, Indiana, where they live. She acts and sings in a local theater group and frequently lectures at schools about writing. She has been a writer in residence at several schools in Indiana, Ohio, and Kentucky. Ms. Gondosch admits that she wrote *Who Needs a Bratty Brother?* in order "...to show just how exasperating younger brothers [and sisters] can be. I hope it also shows that love between siblings is ultimately more powerful than petty bickering."

About the Illustrator

HELEN COGANCHERRY is originally from Philadelphia. She attended the Philadelphia College of Art and has illustrated many books. She loves museums and finds that wherever she goes, she thinks of possible pictures. She is married and has three children and lives in Wallingford, Pennsylvania.